Ionia

(G)Nomes
of
Oz

by

James C. Wallace II
Royal Liaison of Oz
&
Amanda D. Wallace
Royal Liaison to Princess Ozma

Founded on and continuing the famous Oz stories
by *L. Frank Baum*

Scientia Est Vox Press
2016

This Book Belongs To

Forward

This book is dedicated to Garden Gnomes
throughout the world.
They are the Keeper of Secrets,
Defenders of the Yard, and Master Fishermen.
They are known worldwide and beyond, even
into the Land of Oz,
where they are Nomes… not gnomes.
Who can tell the difference?

List of Chapters

Chapter 1
The Dark Side Of The Moon

I t had been over a century since Mr. Tinker had built his
ladder to the Moon in hopes of picking stars for King
Pastoria's crown; only to find the Moon so lovely a
place that he had pulled up his ladder and decided to
make his home there.

During that time, he watched as men from Earth in very strange vehicles came flying around his home.

He pondered in amazement as a number of those strange craft would split in two, allowing one part to actually land on the surface and men would get out and take a look around. He was amazed by the strange clothing they wore and how they bounced around, picking up rocks, saluting flags and even playing golf.

Then there was that one time when one of those very strange craft landed near his home in Mare Imbrium, which he knew as the Sea of Rains, even though it had never rained there since his arrival.

What made the visit by the oddly dressed men from Earth very odd was the even stranger vehicle they left behind, much like a horseless carriage, which Mr. Tinker discovered could allow him to travel great distances across Mare Imbrium.

Now, Mr. Tinker found himself looking down at the lovely blue planet where his former life in the Land of Ev had once been.

He wondered to himself how things were in the nearby Land of Oz. How well had the reign of King Pastoria been all these years? He was even more curious about how Tik-Tok; the Mechanical Army of Oz, who he and Mr. Smith had had invented long ago, was doing. Had his mechanical works remained in good working condition, or was he now only a pile of rusting gears, wheels and cogs?

And of course, there was the whereabouts of Mr. Smith, his partner at the inventing firm of Smith & Tinker. He had not seen Mr. Smith since that day he pulled up the ladder.

The visit by the men from Earth and the mechanical devices they left behind had rekindled his curiosity and his desire to revisit the Land of Ev.

He looked down at the gray dirt beneath his feet and longed to see color once again. With the exception of the blues, greens, browns and whites of the planet Earth

11

which crossed the skies above Mare Imbrium every twenty eight days, much like the Moon had done when he lived in Oz, the only color to be found on the Moon was gray. Be it charcoal gray, light gray or dark gray, the color of his home was gray.

It was odd to him that the lack of color would suddenly, after all these years, hit him hard, like a yellow brick.

He found that he truly missed seeing the Great Rainbow of Oz, as well as Polychrome, Daughter of the Great Rainbow.

Mr. Tinker adjusted the control button on the little silver box which controlled the size of the air bubble that surrounded him and served as his means of breathing while living on the Moon. The bubble grew a little bit bigger and Mr. Tinker reached down and grabbed a handful of gray, lifeless dirt. He watched as the gray soil slowly ran through his fingers and down onto the gray surface beneath his feet.

"What would Mr. Smith think of my little device?" he had often thought to himself. The little silver box was indeed quite a feat of mechanical ingenuity and Mr. Tinker was certain the oddly dressed men from Earth would have loved to get their heavily gloved hands on his device.

He recalled how he had nearly suffocated upon his first try at climbing his ladder to the Moon when he first discovered that the higher he climbed, the less air there was to breath, until he found himself nearly blue in the face and had to make a very quick decent back into Ev.

On his second attempt, he had created a bubble of air which he thought would work well, only to discover that as he approached the Moon, his breathing made the air inside the bubble stale and un-breathable.

Only after much thought did Mr. Tinker finally come upon a means of providing fresh air within the bubble that he depended upon if he was going to visit the Moon and accomplish his goal of picking stars for King Pastoria's crown. He had called it his "Breather-rator" and it worked very well, at least as long as the small copper tank that contained air from Ev remained filled.

Fortunately for Mr. Tinker, his first journey to the Moon found him wandering the South Pole, where he found that by digging into the soil just a little bit, he would come upon ice.

This was so because comets had crashed there long ago and the craters they made at the South Pole of the Moon had never seen sunlight, so the ice from the comets never melted... ever!

Mr. Tinker, being an ingenuous sort of fellow, discovered that he could place chunks of the comet ice into the small copper tank, and by tinkering around with the mechanics of his "Breather-rator" and placing a couple of metal plates that he found attached to an odd metal device which looked like a large mechanical bug that had apparently landed elsewhere on the Moon, into the copper tank, he could turn the ice into water and then the water would somehow turn into two types of gas.

One gas he could breath, which he assumed was air and the other was some sort of gas which burned easily when lit. Of course, Mr. Tinker didn't know about Hydrogen and Oxygen, which are the two gases that, when combined, make water. He only knew that could breathe one gas and use the other gas for heat and to power his new home on the Moon.

It was then that Mr. Tinker, awestruck by the apparent beauty of the Moon, decided to leave Earth and Ev… and Oz behind; and live on the Moon.

When men from Earth had left behind their horseless carriage, it had made his life on the Moon much easier, especially when it came to gathering ice from the South Pole.

No longer did he have to walk for days just to get there. Now, he could do it in a matter of hours.

Still though, after many years of living on the Moon, the longing for color gnawed heavily at Mr. Tinker's soul, as did his desire to check up on the condition of Tik-Tok and find his old friend and partner, Mr. Smith.

As he contemplated the conundrum of which he found himself in, Mr. Tinker found himself thinking about rainbows and green grass, the road of yellow brick, of blue skies and the clear, cool waters of Oz.

The small dwelling that he had carved out of the mountainside which bordered Mare Imbrium seemed dull and drab compared to his memories and sadness overwhelmed the lonely tinker from Ev.

As he often did when times like this overcame him, Mr. Tinker went about tinkering upon the mechanical devices that he had created from the remnants that the men from Earth had left behind. He was nearly finished repairing a minor fault within the "Breather-rator" which had left him without heat during the last sunset when his screwdriver slipped and tore across the dull copper surface, leaving a tiny fine scratch in the metal and a hiss of steam emitting from it.

Mr. Tinker watched as a small cloud of steam rose slowly into the shaft of brilliant sunlight that came streaming in from the little window above the small doorway of his home. He marveled at the interaction of light and steam and was pleasantly surprised when the sunlight, passing through the water vapor, created a small rainbow arcing across the back wall.

As he stared at the arc of colors splashing across the drab, gray surface of rock, his mind began wandering, as it often did when inspiration was looking for a way out.

"Eureka!" he shouted. His excited shout echoed across the rock walls and bounced off the inner surface of the air bubble which encased his underground home.

The little tinker from Ev ran about excitedly, gathering tools and working out details in his mind. He was coming to terms with the scale of what he had in mind and the thought of it filled him with excitement and enthusiasm.

For many hours, he tinkered here and there, putting together various parts he had gathered over the years from those places where the men from Earth had landed. He had to make a return trip to the landing place on the Sea of Rains, using the horseless carriage, to gather more parts. He also headed south to gather more ice for his grand plan.

Finally, he was ready to try out his newest device, which he was certain would be his greatest achievement yet. He had made all his calculations and felt certain he

16

had all the angles right, as well as the mechanics of what he now called his "Rainbow Projector."

Now, all he had to do was wait for the coming shadow.

Fortunately for Mr. Tinker, the wait was only a few hours.

As he waited, he checked his calculations and felt certain the Terran Eclipse was near at hand. He had seen many of them before and they had never failed to fill him with awe.

Now, he set about adjusting the control knobs of his newest invention, the Rainbow Projector, and filling it with fresh ice. In the distance, Mr. Tinker could see the approaching shadow of the Earth covering the gray lunar landscape with a reddish glow.

He turned up the heat on the metal sphere which held the ice and soon heard the hiss of steam emitting into the flange from which the large bubble of gas would form.

As the shadow drew closer to his home on the edge of the Sea of Rains, he set about positioning the large silver shroud that he had fashioned from the silver linings of the strange craft left behind by the men of Earth, atop the ever-growing bubble that was rising forth from the metal sphere.

As the silver shroud encasing the rising bubble began to gain some altitude, Mr. Tinker attached the cords he had fashioned earlier. These, in turn, were attached to the Rainbow Projector, which was now rising high above his home. It reminded him of the toy balloons of his youth.

Just then, the reddish shadow of the Earth reached the edge of Mare Imbrium and Mr. Tinker realized that the time to realize his greatest dream was nearly here.

Minutes later, the Terran Eclipse began as the Earth's shadow enveloped the entire face of the Moon.

Mr. Tinker played out more and more of the cord tethering the Rainbow Projector until it was high above Mare Imbrium and out of the shadow which the Earth was now casting upon the Moon's surface. He played out just a bit more cord until he came to the marking on it that told him the Rainbow Projector was just at the right altitude for what he had in mind.

No sooner had the Rainbow Projector reached its final destination high above Mare Imbrium when a most magnificent thing happened.

A brilliant shaft of sunlight struck the bubble, which by now was more than a hundred feet across and Mr. Tinker watched in awed amazement as an immense rainbow of light spread out towards the northern region of the Moon.

If his calculations were correct, and the little tinker from Ev was certain they were, the spectrum of colors should spill out just beyond the North Pole, where no one on Earth could see.

He hopped into his horseless carriage, which his Breather-rator now encased in a bubble of air, and made for the North Pole at full speed. He knew that he had about an hour before the Terran Eclipse would be over and he desperately wanted to see the results of his work before then.

Fortunately for Mr. Tinker, his transportation made excellent time and in less than forty five minutes, he was well past the North Pole and looking out upon the beautiful rainbow of colors that were laid out upon the gray, dull and darkened surface of the far side of the Moon.

Mr. Tinker looked back and confirmed that the Earth was below the horizon, so he was now confident that he, and only he, could see the rainbow on the dark side of the Moon.

For many minutes, Mr. Tinker marveled at the beautiful colors of the rainbow which were his alone. His thoughts wandered back to the Land of Ev and the nearby Land of Oz and the colors which he missed so very much.

Just then, the Terran Eclipse came to an end and the splash of colors from the Rainbow Projector winked out, leaving the far side of the Moon bathed once more in darkness.

The trip back to Mare Imbrium and his home was filled with both great joy at what he had accomplished as well as great sadness at how quickly it had ended.

Soon, he was back inside the hollowed-out cave that was his home and the Rainbow Projector had been pulled back down. The bubble of air was packed away in the back of the cave for further use when he needed more air.

"I do believe it is time to return to my old shop in Evna," he thought to himself as the little tinker from Ev began reassembling the long, accordion ladder which had been packed away over a century ago.

Chapter 2
Beneath The Deadly Desert

The gnarly, boney fingers of the Nome clawed mercilessly at the hard soil, digging endlessly in the darkness beneath the Deadly Desert. It had been so for over fifty years and Kaliko; former Chief Steward to Ruggedo, the Nome King of long ago, felt certain that he was reaching his goal of digging his way back into the Land of Oz.

Kaliko was, by most standards, an ordinary Nome with the exception that he had once served as a Nome King when his former king, Ruggedo had been defeated by Princess Ozma and made to drink the Water of Oblivion, which erased all of his memories and desires to rule over Oz.

That had been long ago and Kaliko, along with the remaining Nomes of Oz had retreated back to the Dominion of the Nomes on the other side of the Deadly Desert when the Nome King's plans for the conquest of Oz were thwarted during his assault upon the Emerald City.

Upon their return to their homeland, the tunnel that they had dug under the Deadly Desert in order to reach the Land of Oz had been filled back in by Princess Ozma, using the Magic Belt.

That was long ago and for many years the Nomes of Oz fretted about in their underground dominion, leaderless and without purpose. The great stone throne of the Nome King stood empty within the large domed cavern in the center of the underground home of the Nomes.

They had begged Kaliko to resume his post as the Nome King and take his place upon the diamond, ruby and emerald encrusted throne, but Kaliko was not willing to take on the mantle of command, remembering well how much trouble it had been for him, trying to be both kind and cruel, as a Nome King should be.

As it was, the Nomes of Oz soon began to vanish, one by one, each choosing to dig his way away from the Dominion of the Nome King. Each Nome had sought to find some means of escaping the boredom and meaningless existence that was their lot in Life as Nomes of Oz without a leader.

Soon, Kaliko found himself alone in the mammoth underground caverns, wondering where his fellow Nomes had gone to and feeling quite alone himself. It was then that he decided that he would seek out Ruggedo and convince him to return to his position as the Nome King of Oz and call back all the Nomes of Oz.

Kaliko had found the place where the old tunnel had started and begun digging on his own. The pace was slow and tedious and it had taken him over fifty years to do what he and his fellow Nomes had done in a matter of days. Fortunately for him, like all Nomes, he was an immortal being, or nearly so. Time had little effect on him other than the tedium and boredom that had come with digging for fifty years.

Now, he was clawing through the hard soil when his fingers pierced the surface and a bright shaft of sunlight shined down into the blackness of the tunnel, nearly blinding the former Chief Steward and one-time Nome King.

It took several minutes for his eyes to become accustomed to the bright light as he enlarged the hole enough for his departure from the underground world of the Nomes.

In that time, memories of the Land of Oz flooded his mind as he resolved to brave the world of the "up-stairs" people, as Nomes often called those who lived above ground.

He recalled the little girl from Kansas who had, along with her friends, Princess Ozma, defeated the plans of Ruggedo.

Kaliko also recalled how the Wizard of Oz had transformed Ruggedo into a walnut during that time and how a hen named Billina had provided eggs which the Scarecrow had used in yet another battle in the Land of Oz to defeat the Nome King.

He knew that Princess Ozma had somehow erased the memories of the former Nome King and had chosen to settle him in the Emerald City.

Now, the former Chief Steward to Ruggedo and one-time Nome King was looking out from the dark hole that led into Oz and wondering about the task ahead of him.

He was, like all Nomes, loath to go above ground, preferring the darkness of the soil below.

Nonetheless, he was determined to find out where Ruggedo was and where all his fellow Nomes had escaped to. The only way to do that was to step out into the bright light of Oz and face the world of the "up-stairs" people.

And so it was that Kaliko emerged from the underground realm of the Nomes and into the Land of Oz. What awaited him, he knew not, but he was compelled to find his former king and all his fellow Nomes and thus end his life of solitude in the Dominion of the Nomes.

Chapter 3
Mr. Tinker's Lunar Prank

For the next few days, Mr. Tinker made his plans for a return to the Land of Ev. The ladder, which he had packed away just over a century ago, went back together with no trouble at all. It was a marvel of engineering prowess and was certainly another one of Mr. Tinker's most ingenious inventions.

Recalling how difficult the journey to the Moon had been, Mr. Tinker endeavored to devise a way to lessen the time it would take to get back to the lovely planet that had been his home so long ago.

As he thought about it, he puttered about his carved-out home within the mountainside that bordered Mare Imbrium, gathering various items for the journey back down.

His home within the mountainside was an equally impressive feat of engineering for which the tinker from Ev was most proud of.

Besides providing ample room for living quarters, as well as a workshop that any able-bodied person of technical prowess would be nearly green with envy over, there was the greenhouse off to one side.

In the early days, it had been small and cramped with vegetation. Direct sunlight was the only source of energy for his food source and he had spent over half a century on meager rations.

It was, by means of that sunlight, as well as some seeds and nuts that he had brought along with him so long ago, that had allowed him to grow his own food and thus survive for as long as he had within the strange and almost inhospitable environment of the lunar surface.

His home was designed in such a way that the sunlight, when reflected by polished metal panels which Mr. Tinker had acquired during his sojourns across the lunar surface, would shine deep into the cavernous expanses of his home, including the greenhouse and provide ample light, at least most of the time.

He had found these large panels of shiny metal at various places where men from Earth had landed and left them behind, along with other strange artifacts and the like.

As a result, the size and capacity of his greenhouse had nearly tripled, making Life on the moon much easier to endure.

Now, Mr. Tinker gathered some lettuce and tomatoes for a salad and some time to think. An idea was rolling around in his head and he thought perhaps it might work.

The next day, he boarded his horseless carriage for one last trip to the South Pole for water ice. The Breather-rator was functioning nicely, providing both heat and air to breath, as well as sufficient pressure so that the intense vacuum due to the lack of air on the Moon's surface wasn't a problem for him.

The memory of the rainbow on the dark side of the Moon played over and over as he bounced along the bumpy surface and hopped over small craters on his way south. The thought of seeing the colors of Ev and Oz once more filled him with great anticipation and joy.

After gathering enough water ice for his planned return to Ev, Mr. Tinker made his way back north, passing one of the places where the strange landing craft from Earth stood in silent repose.

He had just passed the place known as Mare Nubrium, or the Sea of Clouds, yet he had never seen a single cloud during the century he had been living on the Moon. It was a strange conundrum to his mind. Why would anyone name these places for things which were never here, he never could figure out.

As he approached Mare Vaporum, or the Sea of Vapor, he thought about the Mist Maidens, who were most at home within the vapors that resided high above Oz beyond the clouds.

He also recalled Polychrome, Daughter of the Great Rainbow and wondered how she and the Mist Maidens might fare in this desolate, dry land.

Knowing that he might not ever return to the Moon, Mr. Tinker suddenly made a hard turn right, kicking up a sizable amount of grey dust in the process, and headed towards the east and the place where the men from Earth had landed for the first time.

Soon, Mare Tranquilitatis, or the Sea of Tranquility was in full view, as well as the strange craft standing alone near a large field of boulders.

He had never visited this place before, preferring to leave it alone. This was, after all, the first place men from Earth had visited and Mr. Tinker had chosen to respect that.

Now, a silly prank had invaded his thoughts and he decided to act upon it.

Coming to a stop about five hundred yards or so from the craft, Mr. Tinker got out of the horseless carriage and took off his shoes. He stepped out onto the surface, turned the knob on his Breather-rator so that the air bubble surrounding him was a bit smaller, thus making him a bit warmer, and began walking towards the strange craft.

As he approached the place where men had first walked on the Moon, he saw hundreds of boot prints from the bulky shoes he had seen other men wearing when they landed and walked about.

There were various odd contraptions lying on the surface. Near the craft was what appeared to be a flag, lying on the gray soil. It had a blue square with white stars in one corner and red and white alternating stripes, although the colors were very faded and hardly noticeable. It was just like the other flags he had seen elsewhere on the Moon.

Feeling kinda sad about seeing the flag lying on the grey dusty surface, he reached down and retrieved it, planting it firmly back into the nearby hole where it had been planted long ago.

He then proceeded to walk over every boot print he could find, imbedding his own footprint within the confines of the boot print.

"Oh, won't they have a fine laugh when they try to figure out why the men had boots without soles?" he thought to himself.

Soon, Mr. Tinker was back on his horseless carriage and heading home to the Sea of Rains.

Chapter 4
Nary A Nome

Kaliko looked about and saw yellow. Not just a little, but a lot. Everywhere was yellow vegetation, be it scrub grass, tree or vine. Splashes of green were here and there, as well as a clear blue sky, but yellow was clearly the color of the day as far as Kaliko could tell.

After half a century of digging in the dark, the onslaught of yellow gave the former Nome King pause to collect his thoughts and gather his sight. He had little experience in the Land of Oz, but he knew enough to go slowly and carefully, owing to the strangeness of the land, not to mention the fact that he was now among the world of the "up-stairs" folk.

"That must be the Deadly Desert," he thought to himself as he looked behind himself at the long line of yellow sand that ran from horizon to horizon.

The last time he had seen it, the Deadly Desert was in front of him.

Kaliko looked about and calculated in his mind that *"north might be the way to go."*

Why, he wasn't quite sure, but he had been going east for over half a century now and any other direction was just fine with him.

Now, he began questioning his judgment as he stood before the slowly flowing waters of the West Branch of the Winkie River.

It wasn't that he was afraid of drowning. Being an immortal being, or nearly so, depending on how you look at it, had its advantages. Not absolutely needing to breath was one of them.

The crossing went fairly well and Kaliko was on dry land once more in less than a minute.

"Is this what "up-stairs" folk call a bath?" He wondered to himself as he stopped at a nearby tree to survey the damage.

The dust of more than fifty years had been washed clean and the former Nome King and Chief Steward to the Nome King Ruggedo looked reasonably approachable... at least for a Nome.

The journey north had seen almost no one cross his path with one exception.

A man riding a goat waived at him from a considerable distance and the two of them never came within shouting distance of each other.

Kaliko was glad for the solitude.

It seems that after more than fifty years of solitude, he was not quite ready for the company of others.

"Unless they are fellow Nomes," he thought to himself as the mountain range of Oogaboo loomed larger and closer on the horizon.

It took a full day to reach the borders of Oogaboo and Kaliko was very pleased to be touching the bare rock of mountainside that now towered high above him.

The former Nome King knew little about the Kingdom of Oogaboo other than it occupied a small corner of Winkie Country where the Deadly Desert and the Impassable Desert meet and that it was surrounded by a massive mountain range that kept the little country completely isolated.

He placed his palm flat against the hard, cold granite surface and felt... felt for something... anything that might feel like a Nome nearby.

For more than an hour did the former Nome King seek out his brethren within the massive stone mountain range that occupied the entire northern horizon before him.

Finally, he gave up, realizing with much sadness that none of his kind were within the stone.

"Nary a Nome at home..." he lamented softly.

Kaliko found a small cleft in the rock and bedded down for the night, not so much tired but disappointed that his long day's journey "up-stairs" had produced no results.

A nearby Lunchpail Tree had provided a nice meal of granite cake and limestone pie and a nearby stream provided fresh water, all of which Kaliko had rarely enjoyed during his tunneling days.

He woke up the following morning with a determined goal of seeking out his fellow Nomes and convincing them to return to the Dominion of the Nome King.

Kaliko followed the mountain range northwest for another two days, stopping occasionally to check the stone for any nearby Nomes.

Each try was a failure and Kaliko began to lose hope, though he had only been at it a few days now. He thought about his choice to conduct his search alone and soon determined that some advice from an "up-stairs" person might help him along.

No sooner had that thought crossed his mind when a turn around the corner of a large column of stone revealed a long cleft in the mountain range, extending inward for several miles.

Chapter 5
Gnorm The Gnome

In a flash, everything went from darkness to the brightness of the outdoors. There was a blur of light and shadow as the small garden gnome felt himself being placed down into a spot next to a white picket fence. The fence was about a foot taller than him and for the next several days, the small garden gnome surveyed his surroundings straight in front of him.

He couldn't recall where he had been or even who he was when he came out of the dark. For the little gnome, it was as though he had just been born, or at the very least, hatched. And worst of all, he couldn't move a single muscle or utter a single sound.

For the next several days, he struggled hard within his mind to recall his name and how he had arrived in this *"lovely little yard next to a house,"* he thought to himself.

Slowly, he found he could move his eyes a bit and day-by-day, he discovered the surroundings in which the little garden gnome found himself.

It was a little more than a year when the little garden gnome was struck by a flash of inspiration; when in fact, it was a bolt of lightning during a terrible thunderstorm.

The sudden surge of energy and light awakened in him an awareness of who he was.

"My name is Gnorm," he whispered in his mind to himself. The hearing of that name shot through the little garden gnome and he sought to raise his arms and shout

out loud, but alas; like it had been since his departure from the box and into the yard, he was rock-solid and not moving a single bit.

For the next few years, Gnorm the Gnome stood fast and silent in his place of honor, which was in the front corner of the yard, nearest the road. To his right was the stone pathway which led in and out of the gate. He was positioned in such a way as to be able to watch both the goings-on of the yard, the road and even a cemetery off in the distance with a most unusual tree.

By now, Gnorm had become somewhat weathered in his appearance. The jacket, which had once been bright yellow was now nearly white and his pointed red cap was beginning to dull just a bit and was now more of a pink color. In his mouth was a small tobacco pipe, which was now also quite faded and unused. Of course, all of his clothing and his little pipe were made of the hardest stone, just like he was.

The one thing that Gnorm the Gnome had grown quite fond of in his place of honor were the daily visits by a Dragonfly during the late spring and all through the summer.

On one particularly fine summer morning, the little garden gnome stood by his fence, looking at the pretty green Dragonfly as it flew round-and-round the yard.

Try as he may, he could not utter a sound or even try to talk to the Dragonfly, no matter how much he wanted to. It had been that way for as long as he could remember.

His face, being made of stone, as was the rest of him, never softened in the relentless pounding of rain and snow and biting wind.

For Gnorm the Gnome, it was a silent vigil whenever he watched the Dragonfly.

Day after day, he wished for the ability to speak, to say something… anything!

"But…" he thought to himself, *"if I could talk, I'd probably never stop talking."*

Just then, a flash of green went whizzing by his head.

Gnorm the Gnome always liked the subtle differences in every Dragonfly that visited him. Each one had a unique pattern, or a beautiful mix of colors, or even just a different sound to their wings fluttering.

"I wonder if they would bring me good luck?" he asked himself. *"I would do anything for that Dragonfly if that were true."*

The green Dragonfly was thinking to himself; *"I wonder if he knows I'm even here?"* as he hovered nearby.

He was certain the little garden gnome was alive, but there was no way to tell as it appeared to be made of solid stone.

"Well, he's not ticklish," the green Dragonfly pondered as it fluttered its wings across the stone nose of Gnorm the Gnome, who was powerless to do anything at all.

Gnorm the Gnome couldn't move a muscle, say a word or even blink an eye, let alone smile, which was bad for the little garden gnome since he was very ticklish.

The green Dragonfly buzzed around the little garden gnome several more times with no reaction. He felt like he was getting nowhere.

"Now I know what they mean when they say 'being stuck between a rock and a hard place'; and this stone gnome's going nowhere," he thought to himself as he fluttered out of view and back to where he had come from.

Chapter 6
Mr. Tinker Returns To Oz

The journey down the ladder was much easier than Mr. Tinker could have hoped for, and in a matter of hours, he was nearly halfway home, thanks to another one of his ingenious creations.

The ladder, by means of an odd collection of gears, cogs, wheels and springs, would extend itself to full length, which exceeded the length of a football field. This allowed for a small wagon with wheels that fit snugly onto the side rails of the ladder, to ride comfortably and at a fairly rapid pace along the length of the ladder.

When the small wagon would reach the end of the ladder, the ladder would retract rather quickly from behind and extend outwards, much like a caterpillar crawling across the surface of a vast, speckle-capped mushroom. The wagon would never need to slow down because the angle from the surface of the Moon to the soil of Ev below made for a rapid, yet steady pace, although it was nearly impossible to tell from the passenger's point-of-view.

It was a unique creation of the little tinker that he had put together from more pieces gathered from the odd craft that had landed near his home.

The small, one-tinker wagon made excellent time and Mr. Tinker marveled at how well the wagon rode the rails.

"A very smooth ride… not to mention the excellent view, both fore and aft," he thought to himself as he looked back at the very slowly receding Moon.

A slight twinge of sadness passed through the little tinker from Ev as he bid his former home farewell.

Looking forward, the rapidly approaching planet before him was beginning to cause some concern.

The Breather-rator was working just fine and the "Tinkermobile", as Mr. Tinker had christened his little creation, was now on rapid approach to what appeared to be Ev, although he couldn't be certain.

The Land of Oz and the surrounding countries, including the Land of Ev, had been enchanted long ago by Queen Lurline, who stands dominion over all the lands of Oz, as well as the surrounding fairy lands, magical kingdoms and realms of old.

Only the bravest, wisest, and more often than not, luckiest people find their way through the mist of enchantment into the realm of Oz.

Mr. Tinker now hoped he was "lucky" as the rapidly approaching planet now filled his entire view.

The little tinker from Ev grasped a long handle alongside the wagon and pulled hard.

Sparks soon appeared from the metal wheel as the wagon and its occupant slowed rapidly in order to keep pace with the accordion-like motion of the ladder, which was now slowing down and merely thousands of feet from the soil below. The air bubble from the Breather-rator rocked back and forth until the wagon and the ladder became as one.

Mr. Tinker opened his eyes and saw the ground approaching at a much more comfortable pace and he let go the breath he had been holding for what *"seemed like hours,"* he thought to himself.

Within a few minutes, the ladder had extended itself for the last time as it made gentle contact with the light yellow soil of what he hoped would be the Land of Ev, which is where the city of Evna resides and from where Mr. Tinker called home.

The little tinker stepped off the wagon and onto the hard soil, making a loud thump as he did so.

At the same time as his feet hit the ground, the large bubble surrounding the ladder, wagon and its occupant, popped.

The "pop" resonated across the landscape, fading off over the far rolling hills, making its way across the whole of Oz.

In the old Munchkin City, everyone stopped to hear what sounded to them "like a popping bubble," commented the Mayor of Munchkin City.

"I hope Glinda's okay?" inquired Margarette Munchkin, who was well known for wearing a lovely purple flowerpot upon her head.

As far away as Glinda's Red Brick Castle in Quadling Country, near the shores of the Great Sandy Waste, one of the four deserts that surround Oz and protect it from Outsiders; the "pop" resonated faintly across the road of red brick that led up to the immense copper gates of the castle and caught the attention, although only briefly, of Glinda; Good Witch of the South and Ruler of Quadling Country.

"Goodness gracious," she declared, then just as quickly returned Her attention to the game of chess She was playing with the Scarecrow.

Mr. Tinker blinked his eyes and shook his head.

39

Instantly, he was overwhelmed by a sense of euphoria and profound relief. His lungs inhaled deeply and he thought for a moment that he could taste yellow.

The rapidity of his decent had not afforded much chance to admire the approaching color, which Mr. Tinker had been so looking forward to.

Now, he was surrounded by lush landscapes and rolling hills, all dominated by the overwhelming presence of yellow vegetation.

The trees were mostly yellow, including the bark. The grass was more of a yellow prairie grass than anything green and lush as he could recall from the Land of Ev. Here and there were splashes of light brown and hints of green. Above him was a crystal clear blue sky and not a cloud in sight.

Mr. Tinker recognized it immediately as the landscape of Winkie Country, which was in the western quadrant of the Land of Oz.

"Missed it by that much!" he shouted to no one in particular as he held up his thumb and finger, which were barely separated.

"Now what to do?" he thought to himself.

He looked back at the means of his transport back to what was clearly the Land of Oz.

The ladder and wagon soon found themselves folded upon themselves, creating smaller and smaller packages until each was the size of a pack of playing cards. It was yet another ingenious bit of engineering that Mr. Tinker was quite proud of.

Placing both in a side pocket of his jacket, he decided that his best course of action was to head for his home in the town of Evna.

The only problem for Mr. Tinker was that the town of Evna lay in the Land of Ev, and if he was in Winkie Country, then the Land of Ev was located directly across the Impassable Desert, which like the Deadly Desert, was deadly to any who touched even but a single grain of sand.

He could see the thin line of yellow sand off in the distance to the north, which was the Impassable Desert.

"Now how do I cross the deadly sands without turning to sand myself?" he asked himself out loud as he headed northward.

Chapter 7
Drago, Dragonelli &
The Dragonettes

In the northwestern region of Gillikin Country, which in turn comprises the northern regions of the Land of Oz, there are a series of mountain peaks that form a circle just south of the Impassable Desert. They are known as the Eastern Peaks.

Within these peaks lies a crystal clear spring from which a small lake resides. It is known as Nogard Lake and from it flows one of the numerous streams which feed the Munchkin River.

Nearby is a large castle on top of a small hill, which coincidentally is named Nogard Castle.

However, to call it a castle is a bit misleading as it is more a natural formation of stones that just happen to look remarkably like a castle.

Beneath Nogard Castle lives a very gentle Dragon named Drago and his mate, Dragonelli, along with a half a dozen Dragonettes. Like all Dragons in Oz, they lives beneath the surface of Oz, coming out only to eat or, as was the case with Drago, to tell tales to the children who often gathered outside the massive stone entrance of the castle.

It seems that, unlike most Dragons either in or out of Oz, Drago was a kind and gentle Dragon, by all the standards of the time, although he could be temperamental at times, as all Dragons can be from time to time.

He was also well known by the children of the region for his wondrous tales of adventure and joy. In fact, more often than not, Drago would go on for hours and hours with the children never tiring of his endless tales.

Fortunately, Drago was well over five thousand years old and had been in many an adventure during those fifty centuries.

His mate, Dragonelli was also a very kind and gentle Dragon of just over twenty five hundred years of age, who preferred the peace and quiet of the lower caverns within Castle Nogard. Rarely would she peak her scaly head above ground except in times of hunger or curiosity.

The Dragonettes however, were a rowdy cluster of half a dozen female Dragons, each no more than a hundred years of age or so.

All six of them were loud and boisterous, choosing to argue at the drop of a scale, be it with one or all of each other's sister Dragons.

Dragonelli had spoken years ago to a fellow mother Dragon of Dragonettes, who explained to her that she had solved the argument problems of her daughters by tying their tails to rocks within her own cave.

It took no time at all for Dragonelli to decide that she would not confine her children in such a manner, preferring that they roam free and be allowed to express themselves.

It did however; make for a very loud time in the lower cavern she called The Nursery, which would explain why Drago spent so much time with the children who lived on the surface.

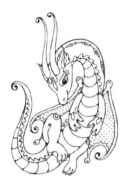

Now, it wasn't that Drago disliked his own Dragonettes, for he loved them very much. It was just that the children who gathered outside the massive stone entrance of the castle were just a tad bit quieter, and given the massive size of his ears, every little bit helps.

The other thing he enjoyed was playing with the children. Their favorite game was gathering the scales that were strewn about the courtyard, then climbing up his back and sliding down his neck upon the scales, much like a giant slide. They would climb and slide for hours upon hours, late into the afternoon until their parents would come for them.

All the Dragonettes ever did was quarrel about this and that... and even some of the other. And yet, he loved them with all the heart one Dragon could muster.

He was also very grateful for Dragonelli, who had chosen to spend her life, raising the family and being with Drago. The security of Love and family had given Drago the courage to face the world above with grace and humility.

Not bad for a young Dragon of only five thousand years, with a loyal and loving mate and six Dragonettes.

Chapter 8
The Royal Magician Of Oz
Goes Fishing

In the high mountains that tower over the northern border of Gillikin Country of Oz lives a young boy, nearly twelve years of age, along with his mother and father, as well as his great grandfather.

What makes this family unique, even among the oddities found in the Land of Oz, is their magical background and connection to the ancient fairy lands which make up Oz, the four desert barriers which surround the Land of Oz and offer death to all who touch but a single grain of sand, as well as the Dominion of the Nomes, the Land of Ev, and many others. All of these ancient fairy lands are then surrounded by the Nonestic Ocean, which both shields and protects these lands and ocean from the Great Outside, which is where you are now, reading this tale.

The great grandfather was the original Wizard of Oz, a carnival magician and one-time humbug who had arrived in Oz well over a hundred and twenty years ago and promptly, with the aid of Mombi, an old crone of a sorceress, usurped King Pastoria and took the thrown for his own. He paid Mombi with, among other items, the King's daughter, Ozma, making the old crone promise to keep her hidden away so she could not claim the Throne of Oz for Herself.

It was the Wizard of Oz who commissioned the building of Emerald City and who, after many years of rule, was discovered and shamed by Dorothy and her three friends, the Scarecrow, Tin Woodman and the Cowardly Lion… and Toto too!

Fortunately for all concerned, Oscar Zoroaster Diggs, also known as the Wizard of Oz, who had accidently escaped the Land of Oz in his hot air balloon while trying to return Dorothy and Toto to Kansas, only to leave them behind; had returned to Oz in yet another hot air balloon ascension which went astray and landed in a great crack in the earth that had been caused by an earthquake.

In Oscar's absence, the Scarecrow ruled for a time, losing and regaining the Throne of Oz before eventually resigning when it was discovered that a young boy named Tip, who had served as servant and slave to Mombi, was in fact, Princess Ozma transformed. As the King's Daughter, She was the rightful heir to the Throne of Oz.

Upon Her restoration, Princess Ozma began Her rule as Royal Sovereign and Ruler of Oz. She retained the services of O.Z. Diggs as Royal Magician of Oz and permitted him the privilege of performing magic, which only two other were granted, those being Princess Ozma Herself and Glinda; Good Witch of the South and Ruler of the Quadling Country, in the south of Oz.

After a hundred years of service as the Royal Magician of Oz, O.Z. Diggs had requested to retire, and Princess Ozma, being a benevolent ruler, granted his request.

It should be noted that in the Land of Oz, no one ever grows old, nor do they die, unless they are destroyed in some great calamity or horrible accident, none of which have happened in a very long time. This was by decree of Queen Lurline Herself long ago.

The young boy of nearly twelve years of age by the time he chose to live in Oz a number of years ago, along with his parents, James and Amanda Diggs, were occupants of the massive home high upon the mountaintops, alongside O.Z. Diggs.

For James Diggs, father of the young boy, his magical background was limited to sleight-of-hand effects and minor illusions, with no true ability to perform actual magic. The young boy's mother, Amanda Diggs had no interest in performing magic as she was too busy keeping her brood, as she called her husband and son, from getting into trouble.

It was young Jamie Diggs, who had demonstrated his magical abilities while fighting the Sycamore and its Army of the Fighting Trees during his first visit to Oz.

When he returned to Oz, the Battle of the Shadow Demon proved his courage, ingenuity and compassion as a magician.

His third trip into the Land of Oz and the gentle defeat of Cobbler the Dog, who had been possessed by the Spirit of the Wicked Witch of the East, earned him the title and role as the new Royal Magician of Oz.

It was he who had inherited his great grandfather's true magical talents and it was he who succeeded his great grandfather as the new Royal Magician of Oz.

Now, Jamie Diggs was looking through his great grandfather's Magic Telescope, which allowed him to look anywhere in Oz, or even the Great Outside, depending on which crystal lens was in place within the telescope tube.

For the moment, it was the diamond crystal lens which permitted the Magic Telescope to see beyond the Land of Oz and into the Great Outside.

"There's our old house!" Jamie cried out. His excitement caught on quickly and the rest of the family gathered about to take a look at the old Hoosier farmhouse in Indiana where they used to live.

Both James and Amanda looked for a time, then backed away, each of them content with their own choice to remain in Oz permanently. The lure of returning to the Great Outside, where Indiana was located, had faded almost immediately after their settlement in Oz.

"They added a white picket fence," Jamie observed. "And what is that thing standing in the corner of the front yard?"

O.Z. Diggs peered into the eyepiece of the brass telescope he had created many years before when he decided to retire and needed to find a family member who could succeed him as Royal Magician of Oz.

"I have no idea..." the old man muttered.

50

This caught the attention of James, who stopped in his tracks and returned to the Magic Telescope.

"Let me take a look, please," James requested.

He hummed a bit and adjusted the focus as the Magic Telescope appeared to be pointed halfway up into the sky.

Of course, being a Magic Telescope, it saw only what the viewer wanted to see. In this case, it was the old farmhouse in rural Indiana, near an old cemetery with a tree-in-the-road and a covered bridge off in the distance.

"You're right, that fence is new," James said. "And I think I know what that thing is you saw standing in the front yard."

Amanda joined in the curiosity and took a look as well. She confirmed what her husband had seen.

"It's a garden gnome," Amanda explained. "A little creature made of stone, with a pointy hat and usually holding something."

"A Nome?" Jamie said cautiously. He had heard of Nomes from many of the citizens of Oz, but he had never seen one before.

"No, not a Nome... A gnome," his mother said kindly.

"You mean a Nome?" Jamie inquired once more.

"No, I mean a gnome," his mother replied matter-of-factly.

The Royal Magician of Oz stood there, perplexed, puzzled and peculiar about the Nome... or was it gnome?

"What's the difference?" He asked his mother.

Amanda Diggs shook her head in disbelief.

"The letter G, of course!" she exclaimed.

"What's that got to do with anything?" Jamie debated back.

Amanda smiled and chuckled to herself.

"You spell knife with a K, don't you?" Amanda asked her son.

James & Amanda's only son stood there, puzzling over his mother's riddle until, as they say, the proverbial light bulb lit up.

Jamie Diggs smiled back at his mother and whispered his magic words.

"Wham… bam… alikazam," he whispered, "light bulb."

In an instant, a fully lit light bulb appeared over his mother's head.

With a look of gentle humor, He shook his head at his mother as she brushed it away with a gentle laugh. It soon popped like a softly floating bubble.

O. Z. Diggs, who had been watching the whole scene with his son, James by his side, laughed the loudest at his family's silliness.

Jamie returned to gazing through the eyepiece, examining every detail of the garden gnome as he considered why the K and the G were silent. He pondered another thought, then asked the Magic Telescope if there were any other garden gnome nearby.

The Magic Telescope barely moved, but Jamie could see that he was now looking into the front yard of a small house in a small block of a small city.

There, standing as still and rock-solid as the first garden gnome was another one. Unlike the garden gnome at his old home, which was smoking a small pipe, this one was fishing by a small cement pond and surrounded by what he thought might be pink flamingos.

Just then, a silly thought crossed his mind and the young magician focused on the fishing gnome.

"Wham… bam… alikazam," he whispered softly, "Gnibble, gnibble."

No sooner had the Royal Magician of Oz uttered the magical phrase when the fishing pole of the garden gnome began bobbing up and down.

He chuckled as the garden gnome stood there, rock-solid and unable to haul in his catch.

"Reel it in…" Jamie whispered to himself. "Reel it in…

O.Z. Diggs chuckled to himself, fairly certain that he knew what his great grandson was up to.

"And just what are you up to, young man?" his mother asked as she brushed him aside to take another look.

"What a beautiful Dragonfly there by that fishing gnome," she said as she watched to fishing pole bob up and down several more times.

"Awww, you scared it away with your silly magic trick," she declared.

With that phrase, O.Z. Diggs and his great grandson stood proudly and faced Amanda.

"My good woman," Oscar declared. "Tricks are for charlatans..."

"And those up to no good!" Jamie continued, recalling the great words his old mentor of magic, The Duke had once declared during the monthly magic club meetings back in Indiana.

"That was merely an act of legerdemain," his great grandfather finished.

There was a general chuckle of laughter throughout the group and Amanda sighed softly.

"I feel sorry for that little fishing gnome," she said gently.

"Why?" Jamie asked.

"Because, being made of stone, he'll never be able to tell the tale of the one that got away," Amanda said with a hint of joy at the pun she had just created.

"Argh!" James cried out at his wife's pun.

Soon, lunch was ready and the Diggs family sat down for some welcomed Potato Soup.

Chapter 9
What's A Wizard Of Oz?

What should have taken an hour took Mr. Tinker nearly four as he trudged slowly towards the desert sands in the distance. In his excitement and enthusiasm following his return from the Moon, the little tinker from Ev had neglected to notice one very important fact.

"Why is everything so heavy?" he thought to himself over and over while the yellow countryside slowly gave way to his heavy, plodding footsteps northward.

He thought about his time before leaving for the Moon and a memory of his first days upon arriving at his lunar destination crossed his mind.

"Why, I was light as a feather back then!" he exclaimed thoughtfully. With each step, he relived those early days and his excitement at being on the Moon. In time, he realized, his body had gotten used to being "light as a feather," and he reasoned to himself that since the Moon was smaller than all of Oz and Ev put together, it stood to reason that everything must be lighter, thus it made sense why everything felt heavier now.

"I only hope I get used to being heavier," he said out loud to no one in particular.

The abundance of yellow, both in the local vegetation all around him and the surrounding countryside off in the distance soon took his mind off of his heavy footsteps.

Now, Mr. Tinker was standing before the bright yellow sands of the Impassable Desert.

The weariness of the journey convinced him that he should make camp here by the desert sands and give thought to his next move.

Fortunately for Mr. Tinker, a small gathering of rocks and moss made for a nice enclosure from whence he could build a fire.

Within the satchel that he carried alongside his haversack, there were many tools of his trade, including a very old fire striker of steel and flint.

In no time, Mr. Tinker had a nice little fire going. The crackle of flames and the sputtering of wood was a sound he had not heard in well over a hundred years.

It suddenly dawned on the little tinker from Ev that was he was no longer dwelling in his far away lunar home. The little cavern that he had carved out so long ago, with all its little rooms and purposes, now sat silent in the cold dark of the lunar night.

For several hours did he marvel at the color surrounding him, even if it was mostly yellow. The sage grass, brush and small trees all appeared in varying shades of yellow. He was glad to see the water from a nearby small stream was a pale blue color, as all water he remembered should be.

He smelled the surroundings at every opportunity, as well as feeling the textures all around him.

After more than a hundred years, Mr. Tinker was glad to be back from his lunar sojourn.

The sun was getting lower in the eastern sky as Mr. Tinker saw the approach of a man riding in a small wagon, which was being pulled by a gray goat with a long grey beard

"Greetings, friend... and stranger," shouted the man as he dismounted the small wagon and approached Mr. Tinker.

"Greetings," came Mr. Tinker's reply. He bowed before the man and goat, which had now joined them.

The man chuckled and winked at the gray goat with the long grey beard.

"The name's Joe Merchant," the man said, doffing a small, red velvet fez, complete with a dangling red tassel.

On the front of the fez, in faded gold thread, stood the outline of the letter O.

"I come from nearby Oogaboo and I am making my way eastward till I reach the Upper North Branch of the Munchkin River. There's a small village with a dock that I do much commerce with," he explained.

"The name's Tinker... Mr. Tinker, of Ev," came Mr. Tinker's reply. Once again, he bowed deeply and the goat snorted a bit of a chuckle under his breath.

"A pleasure to meet you, kind sir," Joe Merchant responded. "You seem a bit set in your ways of old, if I may venture?"

A stern look of puzzlement came over the tinker's face and Joe Merchant could tell Mr. Tinker didn't understand.

"It's just that no one bows anymore," he explained.

Mr. Tinker thought about it for a moment or two and realized that after more than a century, bowing probably had gone out of style.

Mr. Tinker looked down at the gray goat with the long grey beard and started to ask a question.

"Before you ask," Joe Merchant interrupted, "I should tell you that he don't choose to speak. At least he hasn't spoken to me yet… and we've done business together for over twenty years!"

Just then, the sun made a mad dash for the approaching horizon and was soon a mere memory of light and long shadows.

Once the sunset had been appreciated, Joe Merchant offered his services as host and chef as payment for a place to bed down for the night and for the "fine company of a new friend."

The meal was spectacular, as least as far as Mr. Tinker was concerned. Of course, he hadn't eaten a proper terrestrial meal in well over a hundred years.

"Your vegetable soup was amazing!" he declared. This had the effect of embarrassing the merchant man, who turned a bright shade of red.

"Please sir, it's just a simple stew," he tried to explain.

Mr. Tinker then explained over the next half an hour or so about his life on the Moon and his time prior to his lunar sojourn. He spoke of rainbows and the dark side of the Moon, of men playing golf in the strangest of outfits. There were tales of a mechanical army he and Mr. Smith once built named Tik-Tok and an iron giant, both of whom Joe Merchant knew well. He talked about missing the simple things, like the color of a rainbow and the sound of running water.

"If you've been gone as long as you say, then you've missed all the fun," Joe Merchant exclaimed.

Mr. Tinker only nodded in sad agreement.

As the sky turned slowly above them, Joe Merchant told Mr. Tinker the tales he heard during his numerous travels across the Land of Oz. He spoke of a witch-slaying girl from someplace called Kansas, and how she had become a Princess of Oz. There were tales of patchwork girls and glass cats...

"Wait just moment, if you please kind sir," Mr. Tinker interrupted. "Could you please explain to me... What's a Wizard of Oz?"

Chapter 10
The Garden Gnome Gets A Gnibble

The small garden gnome stood firmly at his post in the front yard of the small suburban home, as he had done for many, many years now. His fishing pole, which was no more than a tree branch with some string and a hook, had been stationed over the small cement pond for as long as he had been there.

Nearby stood several plastic pink flamingos, which had been a recent addition to his domain. The paint on them had yet to fade and they were clustered together in a small group near the cement pond.

Across the street from his vigil, he could see the larger brick home where the other garden gnome stood as proud and firm as he had always been. As best as he could recall, that garden gnome had been there as long as he had.

Both had seen many a bright sunny day; thunderous storms with ragged bolts of lightning and heavy rain; snowstorms so fierce that neither could see past their own yards; and both showed the ravages of those many years of weather. Each bore faded red pointed caps, the paint dulled by the onslaught of Mother Nature. Their white beards, which were once as bright as the winter snows they had each witnessed, was now dull and as faded as their hats.

The gnome across the street wore a faded red jacket and held a small wooden staff by his side, while the gnome with the fishing pole wore a green jacket, equally faded as his hat and beard.

Both garden gnomes were made of the hardest granite and yet both were somehow quite alive and aware of each other. Neither had been able to muster even the slightest bit of movement, no matter how hard they tried; and so each watched the other in silent contemplation of what the other one was thinking.

On this particularly fine summer day, the garden gnome by the cement pond found himself bathed in warm sunlight and enjoying his usual duty as the local fisherman. He looked around and saw the pink flamingos gathered about in their usual place, swaying gently in the breeze. In his ear, he heard a slight buzzing sound that grew in intensity as a blue Dragonfly approached from behind the shrubbery in the front yard.

It was a beautiful Dragonfly, with iridescent blue wings, an equally shimmering blue body and striking blue eyes that seemed to look right through the painted blue eyes of the garden gnome.

It buzzed about for a minute or two, then landed on the end of the tree branch fishing pole.

Just then, the fishing pole bobbed once… then twice.

The blue Dragonfly flew off in the direction of the pink flamingos and vanished through the nearby shrubs.

The garden gnome stood there, silent and unmoving as always, but very much stunned by the sudden movement of the fishing pole.

In all the years he had been there, it had never once moved… not ever.

Now, it was bobbing furiously and the garden gnome could do nothing about it.

The other garden gnome across the street could also see the fishing pole bobbing furiously and he tried in vain to muster a shout over to his fellow gnome.

"Reel it in! Reel it in!" he kept thinking to himself as a young boy on a bicycle rode swiftly by, tossing the folded newspaper onto the front porch as he had done a thousand times before.

The garden gnome with the fishing pole stood there, immobile and frustrated by his inability to reel in his catch.

Just then, a flash of memory surged through the fishing pole and into the head of the garden gnome.

There were visions of a jeweled throne and a blazing furnace, filled with red-hot flames and brightly glowing embers. Visions of emeralds, rubies and diamonds cascaded through his mind, followed by whispers of a name he did not recognize.

"Ruggedo…" he heard over and over.

The fishing pole bobbed even more as another vision overwhelmed the little fishing garden gnome. It was of a young girl, perhaps ten or twelve years of age, but no more than that. She had short, blond hair that framed a face which seemed more like a cherub than a young girl. Her eyes were bright and happy, yet the garden gnome felt nothing but fear and loathing upon seeing her vision in his mind.

As the front door to the small house opened and the family who lived there came trotting outside, the bobbing of the fishing pole ceased and the garden gnome stood there, confused and silent, unsure of how to make sense of what he had just witnessed.

For several days, he watched for the fishing pole to bob once more, to no avail. Whatever had been caught on his line had somehow managed to escape and he was left with nothing but a vision and a name and no way to tell the tale of the one that got away.

Chapter 11
A Herd Of Dragonflies

D eep in the lily pads and cattails of Lake Nogard, a large herd of Dragonflies were deep in discussion about a great number of things. The buzzing of wings and the drone of flyspeak filled the far eastern portion of the lake where Nogard Castle dominated the landscape. It was part of the daily routine of the Herd of Dragonflies.

From Nogard Castle, the shimmering of the iridescent wings of thousands of Dragonflies appeared to Drago the Dragon as waves across the still waters of the lake. The sounds of wings and voices could be heard for as far as the eye could see.

Where the lily pads formed vast stretches of green upon the water and where stands of cattails formed a labyrinth of fun for the Dragonflies to fly through, a great gathering of Dragonflies were now debating, as they had for years, an issue which had presented itself to them long ago.

Every now and then, a butterfly would fly by and look at the Dragonflies and wonder to itself why the Dragonflies were in such a commotion... and what about.

Even the large turtle who lived in the inlet at the far end of the marshlands would occasionally poke his head up and look at the Dragonflies in wonderment.

Along the shoreline where the marshlands began, stood a large oak tree that had seen well over a hundred years in the Gillikin country. What few trees that chose to reside nearby were dwarfed by the mighty oak, who towered above all but Nogard Castle.

Drago the Dragon had christened it the "Singular Oak" long ago.

It was near that ancient oak, among the buzzing throng of Dragonflies, where Speedo was speaking earnestly with Flash about the Nomes.

"or the lack of them, as you well know," Flash replied.

"We have seen them vanish one by one and wind up as Gnome in the Great Outside," Speedo continued. "I have visited them many times. There must be something

66

we can do to restore them to our world?" His argument was an old one, as the Dragonflies of Lake Nogard had been witness to the Exodus of the Nomes for some time now.

"We need to know who the leader of the Nomes is, and talk to him," a young male named Odon suggested.

"Or her," came a response from the most iridescent of all the Damselflies, who was known as Anis.

The two now started furiously buzzing at each other and the other Dragonflies backed off, not wanting to get between brother and sister.

The Damselflies, who had joined in with Anis, also backed off. They had no desire to get between sister and brother.

The raucous debate between Dragonflies of all manner and color, as well as the Damselflies, continued for the better part of the morning as the rising sun made its way to midday.

At the peak of the Great Sun of Oz's rise above the horizon, the Herd of Dragonflies began their daily races through the cattails and across the lily pads, making sure to circle the Singular Oak on their way there and back again.

Drago the Dragon smiled at the ongoing races he looked down upon from the castle of stones. On his back were numerous children, all playing about or sliding down the scales on his tail.

One young boy had taken a scale that had fallen off earlier and used it like a sled to race down the hills of green grass that stood between Lake Nogard and Nogard Castle.

Nearby, the Dragonettes were playing about, arguing about this and that... and even some of the other.

They had decided it was time to feed and the marshlands of cattails and lily pads were the perfect choice.

Soon, they were approaching the Singular Oak, each prancing about and swinging their tails in all directions.

By now, the Herds of Dragonflies and Damselflies had noticed the approaching menace and all had moved as one, following the shoreline until well out of reach of the six young Dragonettes. They watched as all six Dragonettes made quick work of the field of lily pads and cattails, devouring every single stalk and leaf.

Before long, the Dragonettes were headed back to Nogard Castle, leaving the Herds of Dragonflies and Damselflies in a loudly buzzing quandary of a mess.

Fortunately, the lily pads and cattails would grow back overnight, but you could be certain that the

Dragonflies and Damselflies were not at all happy about the state of their kingdom.

Drago the Dragon, on the other hand, was quite amused by the monthly feeding of his daughters.

"Never harm any of the creatures you encounter, be they large or very small," he had counseled the Dragonettes. "And the land will provide for our needs."

Drago the Dragon was pleased to see the Dragonettes had taken his advice to heart. They were rowdy, but at least they were polite.

Chapter 12
Ozsnobolis

Kaliko made his way along the trail that led into the cleft and soon found himself face to face with a small bronze gate fashioned in the form of an Oz symbol.

Above and also in bronze was fashioned the name of the town that spread out just beyond the gate.

Ozsnobolis

No sooner had Kaliko muttered the name of the town under his breath when a resounding creaking sound burst forth from the gate as it slowly opened... agonizingly slow for even the likes of a Nome.

The creaking sound was abnormally loud and Kaliko surmised that it must be the town's way of announcing itself.

One other thing that caught Kaliko's attention was how the immediate areas surrounding the gate took on an odd, tannish tone, as if the whole area had returned to a time long ago, when color was devoid and the world was like a very old photograph.

Entering Ozsnobolis through the gate, the former Chief Steward to Ruggedo suddenly felt oddly calm.

No longer was yellow the predominant color of the land. Here in Ozsnobolis, everything was either black or white, with an occasional splash of grey or gray. He felt like he had entered another realm… a realm which seemed almost unreal, or even dream-like.

Of course, he had just spent the last fifty years or so, digging through solid rock and stone, so anything was possible.

Kaliko counted seven houses, all of which were somewhat on the small side. One was grey in color, with a white thatched roof. Another was white in color, with a slate roof of gray. Other homes were black, white or grey, all with thatched roofs of differing shades of gray.

Through the small village, as it now appeared to be, wound a gurgling stream of crystal clear water, crossed by several small footbridges. The center of the village was dominated by a spiral of white and black, which Kaliko quickly determined was brick.

In the nearby bushes, he could see the faces of several people watching his every move. They whispered among themselves and schemed to find out the identity of the stranger.

Now, it should be noted that Kaliko, being a Nome, had a certain look to himself.

Most certain of all was his hair, which stood straight up and ended in a point. It was white as snow and often blowing about, given that it was nearly three feet long from head to tip. He had a bit of a squat face with an

71

equally long beard which made him appear to be more hair than Nome.

Overall, he presented an imposing figure, especially considering his vividly red trousers, shirt and long jacket.

The appearance of the Nome had caused great concern among the faces within the shrubbery. They shuffled about and whispered feverously while the stranger approached.

Just then, one of the faces popped out from the shrubbery and introduced himself to Kaliko by means of a small, hand-held chalkboard and, in his hand, a small piece of chalk.

"Greetings, oh red one. Be ye stranger or friend?" Kaliko read as the creature nervously shifted about.

The Nome stared at the creature before him. It appeared to be similar to ones he had seen long ago. But of course, he had just spent the last fifty years in silent solitude beneath the Deadly Desert, so he couldn't be certain.

The figure before him reminded him of Munchkins, only taller, and not as colorfully dressed.

It suddenly dawned on Kaliko that he hadn't spoken to anyone in more than half a century. Of course, fifty or more years is not all that long to a nearly immortal being, but it was long enough for the Nome.

"Friend... I hope," he replied.

The small figure retrieved the chalkboard, wiped it clean with one quick pass of his sleeve, and quickly dispatched another message.

"And what be the nature of your arrival here in our fair city of Ozsnobolis?" Kaliko now read as the figure pointed the chalkboard at him.

"I'm in search of Nomes... My kin, if you please?" Kaliko responded.

There was a murmur among the shrubbery and a general discontent took over.

It felt odd to the Nome and he felt the need to move on towards the nearby realm of Oogaboo, where he recalled that many of his fellow Nomes had mentioned going to before heading off into the Great Outside, where Kansas resides.

The figure furrowed his brow and scratched out yet another message which he pointed at Kaliko.

"We are the Ozsnobs, citizens of this fair city. Here is my friend." He pointed at the now approaching citizen of Ozsnobolis, who also carried a small chalkboard and piece of chalk.

Like the First Ozsnob, the Second Ozsnob seemed disgruntled at meeting Kaliko and the Nome could feel the silent animosity of the Ozsnobian.

In the next few minutes, he was introduced to two more Ozsnobians, both of whom were silent and polite, but distant.

Three more Ozsnobians were gathered together when Kaliko was brought around to meet them. And like their fellow Ozsnobians, they too adopted a silent air of superiority and aloofness, preferring to criticize from afar.

Another odd feature of the Ozsnobians of Ozsnobolis was that each wore either all black clothing or all white clothing and none wore anything grey… or gray.

Kaliko soon realized that the "up-stairs" people he had just met were not quite normal… at least by Nome standards.

Chapter 13
The Gnew Gneighborhood Gnome

The gnome named Ruggedo watched from his spot by the little cement pond as a family moved in just to the south of him, two front yards away.

There were three young children, all girls, somewhere between the ages of five and twelve; and a more rowdy bunch you couldn't have asked for. They were loud, fun and full of joy.

Ruggedo could see out of the corner of his eye what looked like another gnome.

It was being hauled out of a large moving van and placed strategically in the yard so as to be visible to both gnome a few houses away.

Both Ruggedo and his fellow gnome across the street watched as best they could while the roving trio of girls explored the surrounding neighbor, being careful not to go too far and always stay in sight of their new home.

Fortunately, the girl's father had chosen to chaperone them while the mother supervised the unloading of the moving van. As such, the unloading went off without a hitch.

For the two local gnome, it seemed to take forever before the moving van was on its way and all that was left was the new family on the block.

For the new gnome on the block, it was several days before his eyes adjusted to life outdoors and he was able look about.

Within a week, he had found the other two gnome and all three now seemed spell-bound by each other's presence; so much so that all three failed to notice the shimmering, iridescent blue wings of the Damselfly that had been flying circles around all three. It would have been hard under any circumstances to not see the piercing blue eyes of this one particular Damselfly.

"I don't remember seeing this one before," the blue Damselfly thought to herself.

As she approached the first gnome, she could see that it had a faded red coat, a dull, faded red pointed cap and appeared to be holding a wooden staff.

One more try at getting through to this gnome, which was met with stony silence, and the blue Damselfly moved on to the fishing gnome in the faded green jacket, with equally frustrating results.

Now, the gnome, who was sitting on a mushroom and playing a flute became the Damselfly's next target; and in a flash, the shimmering blue Damselfly had alighted upon the flute and stared directly into the eyes of the new gnome.

The new gnome knew that he could neither move nor talk nor even play the flute. All he could do was stand there... silent, immovable and not in the least bit musically talented.

As quickly as the blue Damselfly had appeared, she just as quickly vanished in a blue blur beyond the backyard of the house across the street.

The new gnome stood there for many weeks as the rowdy trio of young girls made friends and invited them over to see their gnome and play games.

Soon, weeks became months as the seasons passed and before long, several years had passed as the young

76

girls grew older and taller while the new gnome sat silently, immovable as the other two nearby.

Chapter 14
Get'cher Goat

"How can you not know who the Wizard of Oz is?" came a stunned reply from the goat, who up till now had not spoken a word. "Although, if you've been gone as long as you say, you have indeed missed all the fun."

Joe Merchant stood there, dumbstruck by the goat's unexpected query.

Mr. Tinker also felt at a loss for words, but for more practical reasons as he had no idea who the Wizard of Oz was.

There was a stunned silence that lingered for a few moments while everyone gathered their wits.

"The name's Get'cher Goat," the goat finally announced. "But you can call me Frank." He took on an air of authority and Mr. Tinker could tell that the goat had earned the authority he assumed. The one thing Mr. Tinker couldn't figure out was... *"Why Frank?"*

"In the early days, before Princess Ozma had assumed the throne from the Scarecrow... and even before the times of the Wizard of Oz, there was King Pastoria, someone of whom you were well acquainted with," explained Frank.

Mr. Tinker nodded in agreement as Joe Merchant settled in for what looked to be an interesting story. It was one he had heard many times before from many others, only now it was from the goat whose voice he had never once heard in over twenty years. Joe too had one question lingering in his mind... *"Why Frank?"*

"Through ways shrouded in mystery, a humbug of a carnival magician found a means of coming to Oz and, being greeted as a wizard by the citizens of Oz, decided to usurp your King Pastoria," the gray goat with the grey beard began. "The new Wizard sought the aid of Mombi, an old and wretched sorceress in order that he might steal the throne for himself. "

Joe Merchant recalled well the reign of King Pastoria, though it had been well over a hundred years ago. Fortunately for Joe Merchant, Mr. Tinker, Get'cher Goat and all those who reside in the Land of Oz, growing old had been banished long ago by Queen Lurline, the most sovereign of all rulers, who held reign over all.

"And though King Pastoria was both kind and gentle as a King, the nefarious plot of the new Wizard and Mombi found the King vanishing in the night and leaving no trace of his whereabouts. Only rumors of his death and nothing more. It was then that the Wizard of Oz came to power," the goat said with a somewhat sly grin.

"And where is this Wizard of Oz now?" Mr. Tinker replied.

"He vanished one day in his balloon, purely by accident, or so I've been told, when he tried to take Dorothy Gale back to Kansas. That's when the Scarecrow took the crown," the goat exclaimed.

"Don't forget that it was the Wizard of Oz who decreed that the Scarecrow would rule in his place should he not return," Joe interrupted. "And soon after, Princess Ozma, who had been missing for the longest time after Her father vanished, came to power and a most benevolent rule,"

The gray goat with the grey beard snorted and stamped his hoof.

"Who's telling this story, me or you?!" he demanded.

"You forgot to mention that the Wizard returned years later, a reformed humbug and friend of Princess Dorothy," came Joe's reply.

For several moments, Joe and Frank bickered back and forth, not noticing that Mr. Tinker had wandered off and was now staring up at the nearly full moon that shone above the pale yellow sands of the Impassable Desert.

Mr. Tinker reached into his haversack and retrieved a small satchel, the contents of which he poured into his open hand.

Just then, Joe Merchant came walking towards the little tinker from Ev and he perked up at the sight of about twenty small orange beads in the tinker's hand. They shimmered and sparkled as the firelight danced through them.

At that, Joe Merchant cleared his throat.

"What are those?" Joe asked Mr. Tinker.

"I guess you would call these Lunar Gems," Mr. Tinker replied. "These were the reason I went to the Moon in the first place... but I guess King Pastoria won't be needing these now," Mr. Tinker lamented.

"Would you be selling those?" Joe inquired, seizing on the opportunity to acquire the rarest type of gem he had ever seen.

Mr. Tinker chuckled and politely declined Joe's question.

"You say Princess Ozma rules over Oz now?" he asked. "As I recall, She was His daughter... and so these should rightfully go to Her," Mr. Tinker said in a sad but resolved voice.

Joe Merchant sighed softly at the lost opportunity, but he respected the tinker's reasons for keeping the Lunar Gems.

"Where might I find the daughter of the King these days?" Mr. Tinker asked.

Joe Merchant pointed towards the southwest where a faint green glow could be seen rising gently above the far horizon.

"She rules over all the Land of Oz from Emerald City, whose glow is visible throughout Oz," he said reverently. Even the gray goat with the grey beard paid homage by bowing slightly towards the green glow in the distance.

There were several more tales of odd adventures about a new Royal Magician who recently arrived and was rumored to be the great grandson of the old Wizard of Oz. Mr. Tinker was particularly interested in a mechanical dog named Cobbler the Dog, who had been somewhat of a menace to the Land of Oz, but was now a pet of Tik-Tok, a creature which Mr. Tinker was very well acquainted with.

After a time, Mr. Tinker found himself quite worn out by the day's events, especially since he had only returned from the Moon less than a day ago. He excused himself and made a bed for himself by the fire.

Before bedding down for the night, Mr. Tinker held up his right hand and made a fist, which he placed in front of him, level with the far horizon. He touched a small spot on the silver ring on his pinkie finger. Just then, a small disc appeared from the ring and opened up.

Mr. Tinker had designed it long ago during the early days of his life in the Sea of Rains. It was a most unique device which he used to calculate his position, using the stars. He had called it his Lunar Astrolabe and he was now calculating his position in the Land of Oz.

Chapter 15
Hot Diggity Dog

The other children sat atop Drago, listening with great intent to a young girl, who appeared to be about eight years old, with curly brown hair and the face of a cherub, as she told her story of adventure on Mount Munch.

"The creature was nothing more than black smoke and a smell that would turn your stomach," she said, all the while looking most innocent.

There were a few gasps as the young girl described a glass cat and Toto, both of whom were "in service to Her Majesty, Princess Ozma." She continued on, explaining how they distracted the Shadow Demon while she rescued her new friend, Buddy.

"And then the Royal Magician of Oz captured it in a cage of light and... poof!" she said dramatically.

For a moment, all was silent, then "oohs" and "aahs" resounded across the Dragon's back.

Drago was equally rapt with attention as the young girl continued on about a mechanical dog that was built for Tik-Tok.

"He named the thing 'Cobbler the Dog' and took it for his pet," she said with some emphasis.

More gasps, even from Drago as the young girl continued her story.

"It set the countryside on fire and we watched from a wagon on a bubble as the Royal Magician of Oz battled that really hot dog," she said slyly, then waited for the reaction.

The other kids remained silent, none of them quite certain whether their new friend was serious about the 'hot dog' or not.

"Was he a really hot dog?" Drago had asked, taking the bait without realizing it.

The young girl smiled.

"He was a hot diggity dog!" she exclaimed.

A groan ran through the group of children, quickly followed by joyful laughter. The young girl breathed a sigh of relief and looked up at Drago, who seemed quite puzzled by the pun.

"I don't get it," was the only response he could come up with.

"You said you wanted a story to equal one of your own," the young girl replied. "Well, was it?"

All the children and Drago himself agreed that it had been a story to equal his own. Even the Dragonettes, who had been listening in from nearby agreed that it was a fine story.

"I've had to tell it over and over so many times that I can tell in my sleep," she lamented.

All the children embraced the young girl and surrounded her with Love and affection, as did Drago while the rest of the day was spent among kindred spirits.

Chapter 16
Kaliko and the Get-Away

The former Chief Steward to Ruggedo was already regretting his choice to seek out advice from the "up-stairs" people. He felt overwhelmed by their constant silent badgering for useless information, none of which he knew anything about. The only sound was the scratching of chalk and the occasional snort of displeasure when his answer was not the correct one.

First Ozsnob seemed to be the least annoying of the Ozsnobs that inhabited Ozsnobolis, at least that's how Kaliko saw it, so he confined his attention to him.

First Ozsnob handed Kaliko his own chalkboard and chalk, but the Nome politely declined and gave them back. He blushed very lightly, being somewhat embarrassed by the fact that he did not know how to write, though he did know how to read. How that was possible has been a long held secret of the Nomes, for it is that way with every Nome that's ever been.

This had the effect of causing the other Ozsnobs to furiously scratch out their outrage at the perceived slight by the unknowing Nome.

> *We don't take kindly to your kind of folk around here*

First Ozsnob had written. He was looking down his nose at the Nome, though he never made eye contact through the thick glasses that sat neatly upon his head.

Kaliko saw that every other Ozsnobs had written the exact same thing as they all pointed their chalkboards at him in unison. He was unsure how to deal with the odd "up-stairs" people since nothing he said or did seemed to appease them.

He also noticed how each one of them looked down their noses at him through their thick glasses. Their noses were both long and thin, just like First Ozsnob.

Kaliko was now certain that he had to get away from the Ozsnobians and so he examined the countryside of Ozsnobolis, looking for a means of escape. Being a Nome, like all of his kin, gave him the unique ability to interpret the geology of the countryside and where fissures, caves, cracks or other anomalies of the rock might hide. He was hopeful a fissure or long cave might make itself known for a quick get-away.

In no time, he could see how the mountains towering all around came together to form the cleft he had seen upon his approach to Ozsnobolis. He was certain the angle of formation between the two mountains would make for a thin pathway that led north *"out of this madness"*, he thought to himself.

The only problem Kaliko could see was the need to go directly through Ozsnobolis to get there.

The Nome looked around and saw chalkboards flashing at him in rapid succession from various Ozsnobs, who were now in full revolt against the visitor from the Dominion of the Nome King.

Kaliko decided at that moment to make his get-away and headed northward towards the converging mountains in the near distance. He had to cross two footbridges and dodge several homes in order to reach the northern edge of Ozsnobolis.

87

The Ozsnobs all followed him for a time, then one-by-one, they dropped off to pursue some useless stray thought, leaving Kaliko to make his get-away.

By the time he reached the pathway that led to northern edge of Ozsnobolis, only First Ozsnob remained.

First Ozsnob reasoned that he had been the first one to meet him and felt he should be the last to see the Nome out of Ozsnobolis. He also wanted to be able to assure his fellow Ozsnobs that the menace of the interloper had been dealt with.

"I bid you farewell, despite your rudeness," Kaliko informed First Ozsnob, who promptly stuck his tongue out at the Nome.

Kaliko promptly turned and made a brisk walk up the pathway that led past the northern edge of town and towards the crossroads which lead into Oogaboo.

It took no more than an hour at the pace he was going before the crossroads came into view.

Kaliko was pleased when he stood before a signpost upon which three signs were firmly attached. One was pointing back where he had just come from and was marked

Ozsnobolis

One pointed towards the path leading west and was marked

The other pointed north and was marked

Roy G. Bivopolis

     As the former King of the Nomes turned west to
make for the Land of Oogaboo on the northern corner of
the Land of Oz, an odd feeling came over him. A powerful
feeling of strangeness, as though something new was
nearby, rushed over him and the Nome turned northward,
drawn towards what, he knew not.

Chapter 17
Roy G Bivopolis

At sunrise of the following morning, Mr. Tinker awoke to the smell of fresh coffee and biscuits with honey.

Once again, Mr. Tinker thanked the merchant from Oogaboo for his kindness and consideration, as well as a wonderful breakfast.

"Always happy to make new friends and feed them as well," Joe Merchant chuckled as he began packing up his gear for the day's journey. "Besides, you've got a bit of a journey yourself if you be heading to Emerald City. No need to start it on an empty stomach."

The little tinker from Ev chuckled a bit at Joe's observation. He packed up his own gear and was pleased to see Get'cher Goat, a.k.a. Frank returning from grazing in a nearby field of clover and heather for his morning breakfast.

"In all the excitement of last night, I forgot to mention that I heard something about a mechanical Army of Oz and his pet dog visiting Oogaboo recently," Frank mentioned casually. "As I recall, you mentioned something about being the builder of Tik-Tok, did you not?"

Mr. Tinker was suddenly thrown into a bit of quandary with this new bit of information.

He had calculated his position and confirmed it last night, using his Lunar Astrolabe and an old leather map of Oz he had brought with him to the moon... and back.

Mr. Tinker was certain he was in Winkie Country and that a journey to Emerald City should take about three days of walking at a casual pace.

Now, he contemplated the possibility of a change in plans, with the Land of Oogaboo as his next port of call.

Joe Merchant and Frank both spoke of Tik-Tok's new pet, which they each described as a mechanical dog. This had the effect of really getting Mr. Tinker's attention. He wondered if Mr. Smith had any hand in the creation of this new mechanical wonder.

By now, the sun was well above the far western horizon and heading upwards as Mr. Tinker bid his new friends farewell. They were heading eastward and hoped to be bedded down for the night in the Land of the Skeezers, which comprised a small portion of the northwestern corner of Gillikin Country, one of the four countries that dominate the Land of Oz.

Mr. Tinker had decided to make his way into Oogaboo and seek out Tik-Tok and this new pet he had heard tell of.

"If you be wanting to get into Oogaboo, your best bet is by way of Roy G Bivopolis, to the north of the cleft," Joe announced. "You don't want to go in through the south route. That's where Ozsnobolis is, the home of the Ozsnobs." He made a face that told Mr. Tinker that the Ozsnobs were to be avoided.

"Beware the Ozsnobs," Frank declared. "There are only a handful of them, but they are an annoying bunch with nothing better to do than criticize everything and sling insults at others… and they are never wrong! Or so they claim."

Mr. Tinker looked at Joe Merchant, who only nodded in agreement.

"They have very long, thin noses and all of them wear thick glasses that they have to look down their noses to see through. They only speak through the written word, never by voice, at least not to you nor I. This way, they never have to look you in the eye and see the truth of their snobbery. If you argue with them, their chalkboards will only get louder and fuller, thinking that they win through sheer volume of words," Frank explained.

Joe Merchant cleared his throat and Frank took this as his signal that it was time to go.

Mr. Tinker waved as the merchant and the goat headed eastward, the merchant complaining to the goat about not speaking to him for over twenty years. He chuckled as he turned towards the west and headed for the mountains on the not-too-distant horizon.

At around noontime, Mr. Tinker found a nice spot for a respite and some time to gather his thoughts. He could see the "toehills" that Joe Merchant had described to him where the path towards the cleft and into Roy G Bivopolis could be found.

"Why are they called 'toehills'?" he had asked the merchant.

"Because they're smaller than foothills, I suppose," came Joe's reply, along with a shrug of his shoulders.

Now, refreshed and tidied up, Mr. Tinker sought out the large stone Joe merchant called the "Hangnail Stone," where Joe had assured him the pathway into Roy G Bivopolis and eventually into Oogaboo started.

In no time, the Hangnail Stone was in clear view and Mr. Tinker looked behind it.

There, in plain sight, was the pathway leading towards a cleft in the mountainside.

Mr. Tinker made his way along the trail that led into the cleft and soon found himself face to face with a small bronze gate fashioned in the form of an Oz symbol.

Above and also in bronze was fashioned the name of the town that spread out just beyond the gate.

Roy G Bivopolis

No sooner had he muttered the name of the town under his breath when a resounding creaking sound burst forth from the gate as it slowly opened… agonizingly slow for even the likes of the little tinker from Ev.

The creaking sound was abnormally loud and Mr. Tinker surmised that it must be the town's way of announcing itself.

Entering Roy G Bivopolis through the gate, the little tinker from Ev suddenly felt greatly overwhelmed by the onslaught of virtually every color of the rainbow… and then some.

No longer was yellow the predominant color of the land. Here in Ozsnobolis, every color was on full display.

The barrage of flowers and green leaves against the backdrop of the town made the tinker pause a moment to catch his breath. He felt like he had entered another realm… a realm which seemed almost unreal, or even dream-like.

Of course, he had just spent the last one hundred years or so, living in a grey, gray world, so anything was possible.

Mr. Tinker counted seven houses, all of which were somewhat on the small side. One was red in color, with a yellow thatched roof. Another was blue in color, with a slate roof of purple. Other homes were yellow, green or orange, all with thatched roofs of different colors.

Through the small village, as it now appeared to be, wound a gurgling stream of crystal blue water, crossed by several small footbridges. The center of the village was dominated by a spiral of yellow and red, which Mr. Tinker quickly determined was brick.

In the nearby bushes, he could see the faces of several people watching his every move. They whispered among themselves and pondered how to find out the identity of the stranger.

The appearance of the little tinker from Ev had caused great interest among the faces within the shrubbery. They shuffled about and whispered feverously while the stranger approached.

Just then, one of the faces popped out from the shrubbery and introduced himself to Mr. Tinker.

"Greetings, oh new one. Be 'ye stranger or friend?" the figure asked cautiously.

Mr. Tinker stared at the creature before him. It reminded him of Munchkins, only taller, but just as well dressed.

"Friend… I hope," he replied.

The small figure smiled pleasantly.

"And what be the nature of your arrival here in our fair city of Roy G Bivopolis?" the small figure asked.

"I'm in search of the way into Oogaboo… if you please?" Kaliko responded.

There was a murmur among the shrubbery and a general feeling of joy took over.

"We are the Roy G's, citizens of this fair city of Roy G Bivopolis. My name is Roy G Red," the figure now identified himself. "Here is my friend, Roy G Orange." He pointed at the now approaching citizen of Roy G Bivopolis, who was smiling broadly as he approached.

Like Roy G Red, Roy G Orange was pleasant and inviting.

"We are so pleased you have chosen to pass through our land," Roy G Orange said warmheartedly.

In the next few minutes, he was introduced to Roy G Yellow and Roy G Green, both of whom were equally pleasant and joyful.

Roy G Blue, Roy G Indigo and Roy G Violet were all gathered together when Mr. Tinker was brought around to meet them. And like their fellow Roy G's, they too adopted a joyous spirit. In fact, by now, the whole population of Roy G Bivopolis was in a festive party mood, happy at the arrival of a new friend.

Mr. Tinker couldn't help but notice that each Roy G wore the color of their name, so that Roy G. Red wore all red, while Roy G Violet wore all violet… and in between. He was reminded of his rainbow on the dark side of the moon and the same infectious joy of the locals soon overtook him.

"It good to be back in Oz," he thought to himself. It was then that the locals, who had been gathered in a group whispering to each other, looked over at him.

"I don't believe we caught your name, friend," Roy G Red said as he approached the newcomer.

"The name is Mr. Tinker," he replied."I come from the Land of Ev, across the sands of the Impassable Desert."

From the gathering of Roy G's came a chattering back and forth as several of them confirmed their suspicions.

Roy G Violet joined Roy G Red and offered Mr. Tinker another question.

"You are the Mr. Tinker of old, from long ago, who has a knack for tinkering about with machines and mechanisms?" Roy G Violet inquired.

A hush came over the crowd of Roy G's as they awaited Mr. Tinker's response.

Mr. Tinker thought to himself for a moment while all eyes were on him alone. He didn't like the thought of 'old', or of 'long ago'. He didn't look old and he certainly didn't feel old, but considering how long he had been away, he had to accept the fact that he was old.

"I am indeed," he replied. "But how did you know?"

Once more, the gathering of Roy G's burst into joyous celebration.

After a time, Roy G Green took Mr. Tinker aside.

"Everyone knows about Tik-Tok, the Army of Oz since his first adventure with Princess Dorothy long ago," Roy G Green explained.

There was a general cheer of approval from the gallery.

"And everyone knows that you and your partner, Mr. Smith built Tik-Tok before that," he continued. "But we thought you had vanished long ago, never to be seen or heard from again."

The gallery agreed once more.

Mr. Tinker explained to the assembled Roy G Biv's about his adventures on the Moon and his return to Oz.

"Although I was aiming for Ev," he confessed.

The Roy G Biv's erupted in laughter.

Roy G Yellow explained that he had spoken to Joe Merchant a few days before.

"He said Tik-Tok was in Oogaboo and that he had his pet dog with him," Roy G Yellow said.

Mr. Tinker was now more determined than ever to revisit his creation and see how well Tik-Tok had held up over the last hundred years or so, and what this pet dog was all about.

"And what news do you have about my old partner, Mr. Smith?" Mr. Tinker inquired.

Once more, a murmur went through the gallery and Roy G Red spoke up.

"He vanished shortly after you did and we've not heard hide nor hair of him... just like you," Roy G Red said.

All the other Roy G's agreed.

Before Mr. Tinker could inquire about the way into Oogaboo, Roy G Indigo approached him.

"Perhaps you might spend the night here in our fair city and rest up before you make for Oogaboo?" he suggested slyly. "And since you're here, perhaps you could look at an odd sort of machine that appeared here more than seventy five years ago?"

Roy G Indigo must have known how to peak a tinker's interest, because as soon as the little tinker from Ev heard the word 'machine', he felt a keen interest in seeing what the Roy G Biv's were talking about.

Chapter 18
Tinker & Nome

The Nome kept a brisk pace as he headed northward towards a feeling like none he had ever felt before. It drew him onward until he came across a small bronze gate fashioned in the form of an Oz symbol.

Above and also in bronze was fashioned the name of the town that spread out just beyond the gate.

Roy G. Bivopolis

Once again, he muttered the name of the town under his breath and a resounding creaking sound burst forth from the gate as it slowly opened... agonizingly slow, which didn't surprise him at all.

The creaking sound was as loud as it had been at the entrance to Ozsnobolis and Kaliko feared that whatever creatures lived here were as obnoxious and annoying as the ones he had just left.

His entrance into Roy G Bivopolis however, was quite different than Ozsnobolis.

The Nome found himself instantly inundated by the onslaught of virtually every color known to Oz.

Being a creature of the underworld, Kaliko was used to the muted tones of whatever colored minerals were about, as well as the darkness of shadows and faint whispers of light. This cacophony of color was almost more than the old Nome could stand were it not for the now overwhelming and strangely compelling force somewhere nearby.

"Now where might they be hiding?" he thought to himself as he scanned the nearby red and yellow shrubbery for the curious faces he expected to see.

Much to his surprise, Kaliko could find no faces behind the curtain of shrubbery. He wandered into the most colorful town he could have ever imagined.

There were a number of houses and other buildings scattered about a central square which was dominated by a spiral of red and yellow bricks. A small clear blue stream flowed gently nearby, fed from a small pond located off to one side. Two different footbridges crossed the small stream, each leading off in opposite directions.

Kaliko saw that each house was a different color, all with oddly-colored roofs of thatch and slate. He counted seven houses in all, each prominently painted in a different color of the rainbow.

*R*ed, *O*range, *Y*ellow, *G*reen, *B*lue, *I*ndigo and *V*iolet were the colors he could identify, especially since he knew of gems and minerals that spanned all those colors.

Kaliko stood very still and thought he heard the sound of distant voices. The overwhelming impulse that had overtaken him earlier was even stronger now and seemed to be coming from the sound of those distant voices.

He crossed the small footbridge leading into the town square, crossing the spiral of yellow and red brick. In a few moments, Kaliko was standing on the other side of town, watching a group of colorfully dressed creatures crowding around a taller, lanky sort of fellow. He could see that the creatures surrounding the tall fellow were quite happy to be surrounding him. Beyond that, he couldn't really tell what was going on.

Kaliko approached the joyous crowd slowly and soon noticed that no one had noticed his approach.

"Ahem," he coughed gently, trying not to frighten anyone.

With that, the creatures all turned and screamed in fright at the sudden appearance of the stranger. They scattered like the mouse subjects of the Queen of the Field Mice when startled by a sudden noise.

Moments later, the tall, lanky sort of fellow was standing alone, next to an odd looking contraption that confounded the old Nome.

"Thank you, my friend!" shouted Mr. Tinker, who was now quite delighted at having shed the crowd of Roy G's that had been annoying him since they showed him their machine. "Thank you for giving me some peace and quiet while I work."

He shook Kaliko's hand vigorously, which left the Nome speechless.

Kaliko stood back while Mr. Tinker walked about the odd contraption, studying it from every angle and perspective.

From what Mr. Tinker could tell, it had two large thin wheels attached vertically to some metal boxes.

Between the two wheels was what appeared to be a *"magnifying glass,"* or so Mr. Tinker thought. Running from wheel to wheel past the magnifying glass was what appeared to be some sort of very thin belt that he was certain he could see through.

On the back were several nameplates, one of which read:

While the other read:

Mr. Tinker looked up to see Kaliko staring at him with puzzlement.

"I may have been away for a long time, but if memory serves me right, you're a Nome, I gather?" Mr. Tinker asked.

Kaliko nodded and returned with his own question.

"You're from the Land of Ev, yes?" he asked Mr. Tinker.

Mr. Tinker nodded in agreement.

"But how did you know I was from Ev," the little tinker from Ev replied.

"Our dominion borders the Land of Ev, and so we have had dealings with people who look and dress like you," Kaliko said. "Besides, I heard from that babbling crowd of creatures the mention of Ev numerous times."

Mr. Tinker chuckled softly. By now, he had noticed that the local inhabitants, the Roy G's as they called themselves, had overcome their fear and were slowly approaching the spot where they had left Mr. Tinker and the stranger earlier.

Roy G. Violet approached Mr. Tinker and whispered in his ear.

"I don't know his name," Mr. Tinker said softly.

The citizen went to whisper in Mr. Tinker's ear once more, only to be waved off by the slightly annoyed tinker from Ev.

"If you wanna help," Mr. Tinker suggested, "how about a meal for my friend and I, and some peace and quiet while I tinker around on this contraption of yours?"

The Roy G's all understood Mr. Tinker's suggestion and retired to their respective houses to attend Mr. Tinker's request.

Kaliko chuckled softly and admired the tall, lanky sort of fellow from Ev for being able to dismiss the Roy G's so easily. He only wished he could have done the same with the Ozsnobians.

"So, what is your name, my friend?" Mr. Tinker asked the Nome.

"The name is Kaliko; former Chief Steward to Ruggedo; the Nome King of long ago," he replied, bowing deeply before the little tinker from Ev.

"And I am Mr. Tinker, from the Land of Ev… as you well know," Mr. Tinker responded.

Mr. Tinker and Kaliko spent the next several hours recalling their past lives and their adventures while Roy G's came and went, each delivering some of this and some of that… and even some of the other, though mostly it was food and drink.

Kaliko didn't mind the "up-stairs" food, though it couldn't compare to his hand-made limestone pie with sea-foam frosting.

Mr. Tinker was as usual, beside himself with joy at the treats he was eating, especially the peanut butter and blackberry jam samiches.

"What's a samich?" Mr. Tinker asked Roy G Orange, who only shrugged his shoulders.

"It's that thing on your plate," he finally replied.

"Oh, you mean a sandwich?" Mr. Tinker said with delight.

Roy G Orange shook his head.

"We have no witches here and the only sand is in the nearby Impassable Desert," came Roy G Orange's reply as he pointed northward. "Ever since the new Royal Magician of Oz replaced his great grandfather; O.Z. Diggs, the first Royal Magician and former Wizard of Oz, who retired a few years ago, we've been calling them samiches."

With that explanation, Roy G Orange excused himself and made for his bright orange house with the blue thatched roof.

Kaliko and Mr. Tinker looked at each other for what seemed like an eternity, but was probably only a few seconds.

"So you've been digging underground for the last fifty years and only just come up for air?" Mr. Tinker said with amazement at Kaliko.

"And you've been on the Moon for over a hundred years and only just come down for air?" Kaliko said with amazement at Mr. Tinker.

They stared at one another yet again, then the two new friends laughed long and hard at their predicament, resolving to remain friends forever as their laughter faded away.

As Mr. Tinker went on and on about "missing all the fun," the overwhelming impulse, which Kaliko had forgotten about in all the excitement, was slowly returning… and now, he was standing right next to the source.

Chapter 19
The Lunar Gems

D uring his conversation with Kaliko, Mr. Tinker had neatly disassembled the contraption and reassembled it using only a unique type of camping pocket knife that he kept in his haversack. It was complete with all manner of blades, tools, spoon, fork, and even scissors.

"I've seen these things before," Mr. Tinker observed. He was pointing out a small motor attached to the metal box which housed the magnifying glass. "But I've never seen anything like this odd type of material that seems to have been spun onto these two metal wheels."

Kaliko couldn't understand a word the tall, lanky fellow was saying when he was describing the metal thing before them. He had no clue what a motor was and only recognized the metal it was made from. For Nomes, the understanding of minerals, metals and alloys was a natural instinct, so Kaliko nodded his head from time to time as Mr. Tinker droned on about working on things similar to this on the Moon.

"The contraptions they left behind drove around, just like a horseless carriage," he explained.

Of course, the former Chief Steward to Ruggedo had no idea what a horseless carriage was, let alone a Breather-rator. All he knew was that something in the little tinker's haversack was calling to him.

By now, Mr. Tinker couldn't help but notice the glassy-eyed stare that had overtaken Kaliko, especially since the Nome kept nodding occasionally, despite the fact that Mr. Tinker had stopped talking several minutes before.

"Are you okay?" he asked Kaliko, who stood there, glassy-eyed and speechless.

Mr. Tinker thought for a moment and was suddenly struck by a revelation.

"Eureka!" he shouted. It occurred to him that Nomes, being creatures of the underground and tunnelers of rock and soil, should have an affinity for precious gems and crystals of unique powers. In his haversack, the little tinker from Ev knew he carried gemstones so precious and rare as to have never been seen in Oz or any other land beyond the Great Outside. He had collected just over a dozen from an impact crater that had happened recently near his home in Mare Imbrium.

Kaliko stood there, mesmerized as Mr. Tinker reached in his haversack and produced a small satchel of white cloth. He opened it and poured the contents into his open hand.

"Behold! Lunar Gems!" Mr. Tinker declared in a rather grandiose manner. He rocked his hand back and forth slightly to allow the precious orange gemstones a chance to catch the sunlight.

The sparkle of sunlight that now cascaded across the Lunar Gems caught Kaliko in its grasp. He was suddenly a Nome possessed by the eerie orange glow that seemed to call to him as it oozed forth from the orange gemstones. It seemed as if the whole world fell away and only the vision of the Lunar Gems was visible to Kaliko. He thought he could hear them whisper... something soft and strange.

Just then, Mr. Tinker realized that something was amiss and quickly returned the Lunar Gems to their home within the white cloth. Just as quickly, the orange glow retreated into the white satchel as well and Kaliko was left breathless and unable to speak.

"There you are…" Mr. Tinker whispered as the old Nome and former Steward to King Ruggedo slowly regained his senses. "You went away there for a few minutes, my friend."

"What happened?" Kaliko asked as he shook his head and cleared his thoughts.

"Something about these gemstones that I brought back from the Moon seemed to possess you," Mr. Tinker explained. "I don't understand why, but I think it's best if I keep these packed away from now on."

Mr. Tinker returned his attention to the odd contraption, now reassembled and endeavored to make sense of it all while Kaliko struggled to make sense of his own unique predicament.

Chapter 20
Enarc Brenkert

"The plate inside this mechanical marvel identifies it as a 'Moving Film Projector', whatever that is?" explained the little tinker from Ev. "I think whatever makes it work is the same stuff that made my horseless carriage work."

Kaliko listened as Mr. Tinker droned on and on about this and that... and even some of the other.

"The thing has a tail, just like the other stuff I found during my lunar wanderings," he said, twirling the large cord that attached itself to the back of the Moving Film Projector. "I wonder what ENARC and BRENKERT mean?"

The Nome focused hard and found that he could put the *"lure of the Lunar Gems"*, as he had told himself, out of his mind… or at least out of reach, for the time being.

By now, Kaliko had regained his senses and saw that his new "up-stairs" friend was fumbling about and seemed to be in a quandary about something.

"What's wrong?" Kaliko asked.

"I need to find some copper and zinc," Mr. Tinker replied. "The horseless carriage and the other devices I found on the Moon had little boxes on them that contained stacks of copper and zinc. Somehow, they made the devices run and work, especially my horseless carriage."

Kaliko saw his chance to make nice with the little tinker from Ev and bide his time, waiting for a chance at the Lunar Gems. The nagging feeling that he had tucked away earlier was safe for now… but he was certain that the *"Lure of the Lunar Gems"* would take hold of him once more, and then the Lunar Gems would be his, and his alone.

"I'll go find some copper and zinc. I'm certain there are some deposits in those nearby mountains," Kaliko suggested.

Mr. Tinker was delighted with Kaliko's offer and called for a meal before his new Nome friend went off to gather raw materials for the device he was trying to make.

Several of the Roy G Biv's pointed out the local hills nearby, calling them "toehills".

Mr. Tinker nodded, remembering what Joe Merchant had told him, while Kaliko stood there, examining the geology of the various toehills.

"That one to the far right and due north is the Tingling Toe Hill," Roy G Green explained as he pointed northward to a round-topped mound of stone and dirt, with no vegetation whatsoever.

"Why is it called the Tingling Toe Hill?" Mr. Tinker inquired.

"When you get near it, you'll know why," Roy G Yellow added. "The very ground tingles beneath your feet... and when you touch the bare stone, it must be what it feels like to be struck by lightning."

The other Roy G Biv's nodded in agreement and there were several whispered warnings among themselves.

Just then, Roy G Violet approached with a large silver platter, upon which was a large serving bowl of steaming hot corn pudding, a stack of small empty bowls, a pile of spoons and a small clay pot full of honey.

Coming in close behind was Roy G Indigo with another silver platter, topped with dozens of freshly baked biscuits.

A cheer went up throughout the crowd, including Mr. Tinker, although Kaliko remained silent.

Soon, every bowl was full and every Roy G Biv was silently eating... and content.

"The sun is well past noontime. By the time you get to those toehills and do whatever it is you need to do to gather some copper and zinc, the sun will have set," Mr. Tinker observed in between spoonfuls of his meal.

"Daylight, nightlight... What does it matter underground? It's all the same to me," Kaliko replied in between his enjoyment of the biscuits and honey. "Besides, if the Tingling Toe Hill is what I think it is, we Nomes have seen this type of thing before."

Mr. Tinker looked puzzled.

"We call it Fluviam. It's like a river that flows within the very stone around us," Kaliko explained. "You can feel it tingling all around you, just like the fellow in yellow said. But it only flows where two different metals are near one another within the rock."

Mr. Tinker was now lost in thought as he contemplated and recalled the odd devices he encountered wherever the men from Earth had landed and visited near his home on the Moon. He decided that they all made use of this "river that flows", which Kaliko had called Fluviam and he was now certain that the Fluviam could make the Moving Film Projector work… or so he hoped.

Chapter 21
The Tingling Toe Hill

It had been easy to part company with Mr. Tinker as he was totally absorbed with the odd contraption he had been working on since Kaliko had met him and never even noticed he had left.

The Roy G Biv's had escorted him as far as the city limits, but none wanted to go anywhere near the Tingling Toe Hill. Kaliko was glad as he wanted solitude at the moment.

In less than an hour, he had made his way along the left toehills until he was nearly upon the one the Roy G Biv's called the Tingling Toe Hill.

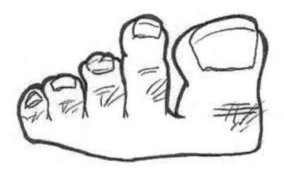

Kaliko stopped and felt the ground beneath his feet. It had the slight tingling sensation the *"fellow in yellow"* had talked about. He had felt this sensation countless times in his years beneath the soil and rock of the

Dominion of the Nomes. It was the Fluviam at work in the rock nearby.

The old Nome approached the bare stone of the Tingling Toe Hill rising above his large, pointed mound of hair. He put a hand out and felt the cold, lifeless rock… only this rock felt alive.

The old Nome put his ear against the rock and felt certain he heard what he could only describe to himself as a humming sound.

Kaliko had never encountered Fluviam this powerful before and the shock of it ran through his body like an electric current. Being a Nome and a creature who dwelled beneath the surface, the shock of Fluviam was energizing, almost to the point of madness.

It took Kaliko several hours to dig down into the stone about a hundred feet or so. His hands, like all those belonging to Nomes, were as hard as steel and could slice through stone as easily as one slice's through a loaf of bread.

It was at about the two hundred foot mark or so that the old Nome came across a perfect description of what Mr. Tinker had described to him as copper and zinc plates stacked one on top of the other in alternating layers. In fact, this part of the Tingling Toe Hill had produced layers of the metal ore so perfectly aligned and in such great numbers that the surrounding Fluviam coursed through his body and gave him a sensation such as he had never experienced before.

The surrounding walls of the tunnel he had carved out nearly glowed from the Fluviam surging through the Tingling Toe Hill. He also noticed that the humming sound he thought he had heard had grown louder as he dug deeper. It was then that Kaliko decided he would gather what Mr. Tinker had asked for right then and there.

He expended a long finger and carved out a cube of copper and zinc roughly one foot square. He then made his way back out into evening twilight with the tingling cube of Fluviam in his hands.

An hour later and Kaliko was once more in the company of Mr. Tinker, who was quite relieved to see the old Nome. He was even more amazed by what the former Steward to King Ruggedo had brought back with him.

"Here you go," Kaliko said as he handed the cube of copper and zinc to Mr. Tinker, making sure the stripes of copper and zinc were lined up horizontally.

"Amazing!!!" Mr. Tinker exclaimed as he marveled at the tingling sensation that now ran through his hands.

Before Kaliko could warn his new "up-stairs" friend, Mr. Tinker had rotated the cube as he examined it and was now holding it so that the stripes of copper and zinc were lined up vertically.

No sooner had he done that when a surge of energy knocked Mr. Tinker off his feet and halfway across the courtyard of yellow and red brick.

"Excelsior!!!" Mr. Tinker shouted breathlessly. His hair was now standing on end in all directions and the Roy G Biv's were all laughing uncontrollably at the odd sight in their town square… or spiral, as the case may be.

Chapter 22
A Night At The Movies

The little tinker from Ev puzzled over the cube that Kaliko had brought him. He was certain it would make the 'moving film projector' work, though what it would do when it did work was a mystery to him.

"It has to do with this tail on it," Mr. Tinker suggested to the old Nome.

"All I know is that when you hold it wrong, the Fluviam really flows," Kaliko responded.

Mr. Tinker furrowed his brow until an idea crossed his mind.

"The few tails I saw on the Moon were attached to smaller boxes which I suspect may contain this Fluviam you've brought me," Mr. Tinker recalled. "I wonder…"

The tinker began disassembling the end of the odd contraption's tail and noticed immediately something very familiar.

"This tail has the same metal strips attached to copper wires in its tail as the boxes up there," Mr. Tinker said, pointing towards the now rising Moon.

The sight of the Moon now rising above the far western horizon caught Kaliko off guard and caused him to gasp slightly. The nagging feeling he had put away earlier began to slowly make itself known… at least just a bit.

The vision of the rising Moon reminded him that the Lunar Gems were *"just over there, in that haversack."*

By now, Mr. Tinker had fully disassembled the end of the tail of the odd contraption named Enarc Brenkert and was moving the thing out onto the yellow brick that was spiraling by in the town square.

"Could you fetch me that block of Fluviam please, my good fellow?" Mr. Tinker very politely asked his new friend, Kaliko.

Kaliko nodded and went to fetch the block of Fluviam that was sitting nearby.

Mr. Tinker stopped and looked up at the rising Moon. His mind wandered back to his long days, and nights, living among the black and white and gray of the lunar landscape.

"*I wonder how my garden is doing*?" he thought to himself and chuckled.

Kaliko retuned with the block of Fluviam and set it down upon a small wooden stool Mr. Tinker had brought to him by Roy G Red.

"Why is that block sitting on top of part of the tail of that thing?" Roy G Blue observed, pointing out the wire that was attached to the seat of the stool, upon which sat the block of Fluviam.

"Ah… We shall see," Mr. Tinker said slyly. He took the other half of the tail, which also happened to be made of copper wire, and looked around for something to hold it down onto the block of Fluviam.

"What are you looking for?" Roy G Blue asked.

"Something to hold this thing's tail down on that block of Fluviam because I'm not touching it again with my bare hands," Mr. Tinker replied.

Roy G Blue excused himself to retrieve something and returned moments later.

116

"Will this do?" Roy G Indigo asked as he held up a small sack of potatoes.

Mr. Tinker accepted the sack graciously and attached the copper wire to the bottom of the sack.

He held it just above the block of Fluviam and wondered if Enarc Brenkert would come to Life.

The next moment, Mr. Tinker released the sack of potatoes, which landed with a small thud onto the block of Fluviam; and then a most wondrous thing happened.

Enarc Brenkert, the Motion Picture Projector did indeed come to Life, or so it seemed in those first moments.

A bright light burst forth from the magnifying glass and the two thin wheels started spinning and feeding the odd material through the gears of the metal box and past the magnifying glass.

By a happy coincidence or perhaps just pure luck, the beam of light that burst forth from the magnifying glass landed on the side of Roy G Yellow's house.

All seven Roy G Biv's were immediately dumbstruck by the odd contraption that had been with them for as long as anyone could remember.

Mr. Tinker was absolutely delighted that Enarc Brenkert worked. The whirring of the gears and projected light captivated the little tinker.

Even Kaliko found the whole thing quite amazing, even though his inner thoughts were focused on the Lunar Gems.

"Isn't that the Cowardly Lion?" asked a voice from the assembled Roy G Biv's at the sight of a lion appearing to roar on the side of the house.

Murmurs of agreement ran through the crowd.

"Who is that girl with the dog?" asked another voice.

Another round or murmurs ran through the crowd as the light flickered across the siding of the yellow house and the whirring of Enarc Brenkert was the only other sound to be heard in the town center.

There was a subtle sound of hissing and displeasure when an old woman came riding across Roy G Yellow's house on a bicycle and even more so when she left with the little dog in a basket.

A roar of approval greeted the little dog's escape from the basket, even from Kaliko, who was now totally engrossed by the sight of light flickering across the house.

"That dog kinda looks like Toto," Roy G Red suggested.

Nearly everyone agreed. Like many in the Land of Oz, the Roy G Biv's were familiar with the story of Dorothy and her adventures in Oz. They also agreed that the thing they were looking at looked drab and dull, with no color whatsoever other than tan, brown and white. The only one who liked the drabness of the projected light was the old Nome.

Mr. Tinker chuckled as he watched the little dog steal a wiener from the old man's stick above the campfire

There were gasps and shouts of concern when the tornado appeared and the house flew away.

Moments later, the girl and the dog on the side of the house opened a door and stepped out into color almost as bright as the ones in the surroundings of Roy G Bivopolis.

Chapter 23
Lions, Tigers And Bears!

"Oh my!" nearly every citizen of Roy G Bivopolis shouted in unison at the sight of the red ruby slippers on the feet protruding from beneath the old house.

Everyone agreed that the little town square looked just like their own, which, rumor has it, was set forth by the hand of King Pastoria. It was He who had also decreed the spiral of red and yellow brick in Munchkin City long ago.

Soon, everyone on Roy G Yellow's house was dancing silently around the spiral and waiving farewell to the little girl and the dog.

By now, many of the Roy G Biv's had noticed a nagging need for a snack while they were watching Enarc Brenkert project the light.

Roy G Violet suggested popcorn, which they had secured in trade with Joe Merchant just a few days ago. His suggestion was met with cheers of approval and the man in violet went about cooking up some popcorn.

By now, Mr. Tinker had figured out what was going on with the odd contraption he had been enticed into bringing it back to Life.

"I understand now why it's called a Motion Picture Projector," he said to Kaliko, who was currently captivated by the dancing scarecrow on the side of the yellow house. "That material spinning from one wheel to another has pictures on it, and when the light passes through the pictures, they are projected up there.

Mr. Tinker pointed towards the light while he continued examining the spinning gears.

"Enarc Brenkert does it so fast that they look like pictures that move," explained Mr. Tinker, if only to himself.

Kaliko listened in as the Roy G Biv's ate popcorn and debated whether or not what they were seeing was a story about Princess Dorothy and her first visit to the Land of Oz while a little girl, a dog, a scarecrow, a tin woodman and a lion ran silently and blissfully through a field of what appeared to be poppies, then take a nap. He tried the popcorn and decided he didn't like it.

Mr. Tinker couldn't get enough popcorn and required several refills of his bowl.

By the time the green witch was melted by the little girl, everyone in Roy G Bivopolis had agreed that this was indeed a magical creation that told the story of Princess Dorothy and her first visit to the Land of Oz.

"The Magic Slippers should be silver, not red rubies," Roy G. Blue observed.

"And where was the Queen of the Field Mice and Her subjects?" asked a voice from the crowd.

"Don't forget the Kalidahs!" came another voice.

There was a general murmur of agreement, but all the Roy G Biv's agreed that it was an excellent way to tell Princess Dorothy's story.

"Is it alive?" Kaliko asked, pointing at Enarc Brenkert. He had heard stories about a mechanical army named Tik-Tok and an Iron Giant and wondered to himself if this was *another one of those bizarre 'up-stairs' creatures"* he had been warned about when Ruggedo was still the Nome King.

"No, I think not," Mr. Tinker reassured the old Nome. "It's the Fluviam at work here, I believe."

Just then, the colors went away and everyone let out a collective groan as the little girl and her dog lay in bed, surrounded by the people from Oz, all in browns and tans and white.

Moments later, the top wheel stopped spinning and the bottom wheel sped up while a piece of the material within the wheel flapped round and round.

The bright white light bouncing off of Roy G yellow's house nearly blinded the populace of Roy G Bivopolis, all of whom shouted in disappointment.

Mr. Tinker flipped a switch on the small black box between the wheels and the bright light ceased almost immediately, along with the whirring sound of Enarc Brenkert.

For several moments, there was nothing but silence and only the light of the still rising Full Moon to see by. Several crickets were having a conversation nearby among the cattails in the stream and overhead, a thin flash of greenish light streaked silently overhead.

"Ooooh," came the crowd's response. "Ahhh…"

By now, several of the Roy G Biv's had gone to light the lamps and lanterns that were scattered about the town spiral and bridges.

A lamp was brought to Mr. Tinker, who accepted it and directed the light towards the Motion Picture Projector.

"I think I can make it work again," Mr. Tinker suggested. This was met with huge approval from the gathering and Roy G Violet went to make more popcorn.

Kaliko suddenly noticed that the nagging feeling had returned and his thoughts wandered back to the Lunar Gems.

"Wait!" Roy G Indigo shouted. "We have to share this with the Ozsnobs!"

Chapter 24
The Ozsnobs

It took more than an hour and all seven Roy G Biv's to convince the Ozsnobs to come over and watch Enarc Brenkert tell the story of Princess Dorothy's first visit to Oz.

By now, the Full Moon was high overhead when all seven Roy G Biv's came marching back with all seven Ozsnobs in tow.

The Ozsnobs, for their part, were intrigued by the idea of a picture that moved, but they were all dead set against the idea that it might, in fact, tell the story of Princess Dorothy's first journey to the Land of Oz. Their chalkboards occasionally exchanged furtive replies to enigmatic questions and none of them smiled.

At the sight of Kaliko, all seven Ozsnobs lunged into a rage of writing and erasing and scribbling mad ravings about the creature with the pointy white hair and the look of a Nome.

The Roy G Biv's found the Ozsnobs quite amusing and laughed often at their exchanges of anger and glaring looks down their noses at each other... and at Kaliko.

Mr. Tinker was quite disturbed by the sudden appearance of the seven people of black and white. In his mind, a vision of the approaching darkness that came with every lunar sunset flooded his senses and overwhelmed the little tinker from Ev. The starkness of the Moon's surface; the division between black and white; of light and shadow rendered Mr. Tinker quite unaware of what was about to happen.

Kaliko had retreated into his inner self as the Ozsnobs surrounded him with chalkboards and glares and always the screeching of chalk upon slate. He tried his best to ignore them in hopes that they would *"go away!"* only to discover the nagging feeling that signaled the presence of the Lunar Gems making itself quite well known once more.

Before he knew it, Kaliko found himself back-to-back with Mr. Tinker and it was then that the old Nome looked over his shoulder and saw the "up-stairs" person who held the Lunar Gems seemed nearly unconscious and unaware of anything around him.

In an instant, something within the mind of the former Chief Steward to King Ruggedo snapped. The sound of that snapping sent shock waves through the old Nome and he realized that his chance had come upon him at last.

Without so much as a second thought, Kaliko snatched the haversack beside Mr. Tinker, causing the little white cloth pouch to come flying out, as if escaping its captor and reaching for freedom.

What ever freedom the little white pouch had hoped for was quickly dashed as Kaliko reached out and deftly caught it in mid-flight. He dropped the haversack and made an immediate dash for the town spiral and footbridges leading out towards the crossroads that had brought him to Roy G Bivopolis in the first place.

Roy G Red had to shake Mr. Tinker for nearly a minute before he came out of whatever it was that had taken hold of him.

Mr. Tinker shook his head to clear his thoughts as the visions of shadows and light faded from his inner thoughts.

"That creature took something from your satchel," Roy G Red exclaimed.

Mr. Tinker knew immediately without looking what the old Nome had taken. He looked about and saw the seven people that had arrived with the Roy G Biv's and saw them for what they truly were; pompous, arrogant, self-centered people with nothing better to do than criticize others who they felt threatened by; just as Joe Merchant and Get'cher Goat had warned they would be.

It was as if a huge weight had been lifted from his shoulders and Mr. Tinker was suddenly invigorated and quickly realized that he had to find the old Nome and retrieve the Lunar Gems so that he could give them to Princess Ozma; in loving memory of Her father, King Pastoria.

As he looked about for Kaliko, all seven Roy G Biv's and all seven Ozsnobs pointed westward towards the cleft in the nearby mountains, sensing that Mr. Tinker was about to leave them.

Mr. Tinker made quick apologies to everyone in attendance as he gathered up his haversack and filled it with tools and devices and items no one there understood. He turned and flipped the switch on Enarc Brenkert, confident that he had taught Roy G Violet how to make the Motion Picture Projector work, over and over again.

It was nearly midnight and the light of the Full Moon made Mr. Tinker's mad dash westward easy as he left behind the whirring gears and motors of Enarc Brenkert, softened by the scratching of chalk upon slate and the gentle laughter of the Roy G Biv's.

126

Chapter 25
The Wackbards Tunnel

Kaliko made quick time of his escape and was soon at the crossroads where the signpost pointed the way. It was a fairly easy choice for him to make as he headed west towards Oogaboo with the Lunar Gems in hand.

Twenty minutes later and the instincts of the old Nome were proven true as the sharp cliffs of the landscape came together and formed a very narrow pathway through the mountains and into the Land of Oogaboo.

Before he could reach the narrow pathway, Kaliko came across a most welcome sight and one he had hoped would present itself sooner or later.

There, jutting forth from a nearby outcropping of rock, was a hole in the side of the mountain.

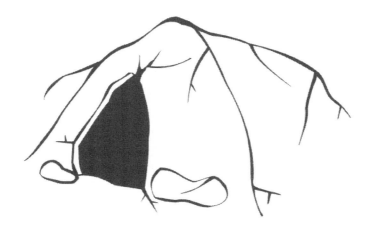

Above the hole and barely visible was a small engraved bronze plaque, which Kaliko could not read.

He examined the opening carefully, parting the cobwebs that nearly blocked the entrance; and with the keen eye of one who was used to tunneling through dirt and stone, he determined in no time at all that it had not been dug by Nomes.

Despite this, he was determined to take the way underground and he felt certain that this tunnel would lead into Oogaboo.

Five minutes into the darkness and Kaliko was certain that he had made a mistake in taking the way underground. For some odd reason he could not explain, it felt like the tunnel was moving. He had never felt a tunnel do that before... ever!

Kaliko tried turning back, but the entrance was nowhere to be found and it seemed as if the walls of rock had circled back on themselves.

Meanwhile, Mr. Tinker was just reaching the crossroads where the signpost stood. He remembered what the old Nome had said about finding his fellow Nomes and turned westward for the Land of Oogaboo.

Twenty minutes later, he came across perfectly circular hole in the side of the mountain and reasoned that, being a Nome and a creature of the underworld, Kaliko might choose this way to make his escape.

A careful examination of the opening revealed dangling cobwebs that had once been outstretched, and a single set of footprints leading through the dust and into the darkness.

Above the hole and barely visible was a small engraved bronze plaque, which Mr. Tinker could not read without the aid of a magnifying glass.

After a quick retrieval of one from his haversack, Mr. Tinker read aloud the following words:

Wackbards Tunnel

Courtesy of Jamie Diggs: Royal Magician of Oz

Mr. Tinker fashioned a torch from some cloth, a nearby fallen branch and some oil he carried in a flask within his haversack.

Soon, he was navigating his way down the long dark of the underworld when he noticed an odd sensation that *"didn't feel quite right,"* and like his predecessor before him, Mr. Tinker tried to double back, only to find the way back had doubled back on itself. He was lost...

Mr. Tinker stopped in his tracks and looked down. In the pale light of the torch, he could see multiple footsteps, each leading in opposite directions, which lead him to believe that... he was definitely lost.

Kaliko thought he heard footsteps in the distance, but the oddness of the Wackbards Tunnel and Lure of the Lunar Gems had deafened him to all things not Lunar Gems.

He stood perfectly still for nearly an hour, waiting for the sound of footsteps to return, but to no avail. It was then that a pale light appeared in the distance of the darkness and Kaliko walked on in search of the light.

In a matter of minutes, the pale light had become a way out and the old Nome soon found himself standing once more in the "up-stairs" world, only this time, he was standing nearly face-to-face with a rather large and rather imposing Dragon... with children sliding down the scales on his back all the way to the end of his tail.

Meanwhile, Mr. Tinker stood perfectly still for well over an hour, trying to determine what he should do. He was used to tunnels, since that was how he had lived for over a hundred years while on the Moon.

Now however, he felt suddenly confined and almost claustrophobic.

It was then that he saw a dim light in the far distance and resolved to make it there as quickly as possible.

Soon, the little tinker from Ev was standing once more in the brilliant sunlight of Oz, looking about at all the vibrant colors and noticing that there was a field of pinwheels of all different sizes spread out before him. In the distance, he could see a small house near where the field of pinwheels began.

Chapter 26
Nomes & Dragons

D rago snorted at the sudden appearance of a Nome right in front of him. A moment before, there hadn't even been a hole in the side of the hill near Nogard Castle, now a Nome was emerging from it. In fact, Drago had seen a number of Nomes appearing and disappearing over the years, and now here was another one to watch pass by.

"And who might you be?" the young Dragon asked. Drago looked intently at Kaliko, having realized that the creature before him was a Nome. He felt an odd sensation, as though he were drawn to the Nome, much like a moth to a flame.

The young Dragon shook his entire body very gently in order to aid the children in getting down quickly and behind him. The children all landed on their feet and with a mild sense of fear at the arrival of the stranger, although there was one little girl who seemed to show no fear at first sight of the Nome.

Unlike Dragons, the local children were unaccustomed to seeing Nomes wandering about. Of course, this little girl was no ordinary child of Oz.

Drago took a very defensive stance to protect the children, owing to his past experiences with other Nomes that had come and gone. That and the fact that Dragons and Nomes have always had a very tense relationship; and this Nome was carrying something unique and powerful.

Since Nomes are creatures of the underground realm, as are Dragons, they often could hold sway over the ancient beasts, commanding them to serve and obey. No one is sure why, but it is well known among Nomes and Dragons... and few others.

"My kind are Nome," he replied.

If it had been pitch dark, as if in an old, deep tunnel, and the old Nome unable to see anything at all, he would have recognized Drago instantly from the intense snorting brimstone breath that had nearly knocked him over.

"And you are a Dragon!" Kaliko shouted with great authority.

It had been well over a hundred years since he had last ridden a Dragon and now, here was one right in front of him. His Voice of Command, which all Nomes posses and use from time to time when confronted with creatures from the underground, had reared up through sheer instinct.

"What is your name?" Kaliko exclaimed in an almost hypnotic manner. He knew how to control Dragons and for the moment, he felt empowered by something unlike anything he had ever experienced before. The pouch containing the Lunar Gems seemed filled with a soft, muted light and Kaliko patted it gently.

"Drago," the large, young Dragon said with great authority and resolve. He too knew that Nomes had some sort of power over Dragons. It was something that connected the underground realm within itself. All creatures of the underground realm are bonded by their connection to rock and stone.

In the last few years, as Nomes came and went out of the Land of Oz, Drago had learned to resist their control; but something about this Nome was not normal, at least not by Drago's standards.

By now, the children standing behind Drago were becoming more concerned and even a little bit scared; all but one little girl, who stepped forward and spoke up.

"What is your name?!" she shouted defiantly at the former Chief Steward to King Ruggedo.

Kaliko was taken aback by the brave question from what he decided must be *"a youngling or some sort of up-stairs offspring,"* he thought to himself.

"Hmmph!" snorted the old Nome as he returned his attention to the Dragon before him. "Kaliko... and I suppose you have a name?"

"My name is Heavenlee and you're mean!" she shouted as she approached the old Nome, then quickly kicked him on his shins, just below his knees.

It was like *"kicking a rock"*, Heavenlee thought to herself. She backed away, unsure of the tall stranger she had just kicked but unwilling to show it.

Kaliko barely noticed her as he reached out to touch Drago's claw. In doing so, Kaliko imposed his will upon the young Dragon, commanding him by sheer thought into taking him wherever he wanted to go.

Drago had been able to resist every Nome that had come his way and gone the other; but with this one, he was unable to resist the control the old Nome imposed upon him. There was something about this Nome... or was it something else?

Just then, Drago curled his long tail around to encircle Heavenlee. It was then just a matter of gently nudging her back until he had all the children corralled and safely behind him.

Heavenlee tried to resist, but she knew Drago was only trying to help, as did all the other children.

In the blink of an eye, Kaliko had surmounted the young Dragon and was now firmly in place upon the Dragon's wings. He knew instinctively that Oogaboo and his path towards his fellow Nomes was due west, by the Compass of Oz.

It should be noted that in the Land of Oz, east and west are reversed so that the Great Sun of Oz rises in the west and sets in the east. Why? No one knows, for it has been that way since the beginnings of Oz and all the fairylands surrounding it.

"You will take me to the Land of Oogaboo so I may find the whereabouts of my kin and kind," Kaliko commanded.

Drago was helpless beneath the will of the Nome... and something else.

Chapter 27
Aadon Blu's Visitor

It took a few minutes for Mr. Tinker's eyes to adjust to the brightness of the countryside. Soon, he could make out nearly a hundred pinwheels of various sizes in the nearby field. Some were no taller than himself while others were larger than a house, and all were blue and white in color.

In the distance was a little house with a small curl of smoke rising from the chimney.

The little tinker from Ev made his way towards the rising smoke and soon found himself standing at the doorway of the house.

Nearby on the porch was a small umbrella, also blue and white in color and on the door itself was a large brass knocker, which he promptly grasped and gave the door several loud raps.

He could hear footsteps as whoever lived there approached from within.

The door slowly creaked open, revealing the broad smiling face of a young man with piercing blue eyes and short brown hair.

"Welcome friend to the Pinwheel Fields!" he declared. "Are you here to visit the Royal Magician of Oz?"

Mr. Tinker shook his head. He hadn't expected such a rousing welcome... but then again, he was still getting used to being around people once more.

"It's a good thing you're not, since the pinwheels aren't spinning, which means the Royal Magician of Oz isn't accepting visitors at the moment," the young man explained. "Besides, you don't look like you have a ticket."

Mr. Tinker looked into the piercing blue eyes and smiled. He could tell that whoever this person was, he had a good and kind heart.

"Come in and relax. You look as though you've been on a long journey," the young said invitingly. "My name's Aadon Blu."

Mr. Tinker walked into a charming front room full of knick knacks and various clocks, none of which told the same time.

"Please, have a seat. Would you like something to drink or eat?" Aadon asked as he gestured towards a nearby rocking chair.

"Yes, please," Mr. Tinker replied as he sat down.

A few moments later and Aadon Blu returned from the kitchen with two glasses of milk and some cheese.

Mr. Tinker was very grateful for the meal and soon finished off his plate of cheese.

"You must have been very hungry," Aadon observed. "Was it a long journey?"

"You have no idea," the little tinker from Ev replied.

He then proceeded to spend the next few hours recalling his grand adventure on the Moon, his return to Oz and the very odd creatures he had met in the last few days.

Aadon Blu seemed particularly interested in Enarc Brenkert and the moving film it projected.

"I've met Dorothy before and she has described to me her adventure when she first came to Oz," Aadon said. "I wonder if this thing you describe is anything like what she has told me?"

Mr. Tinker just shrugged his shoulders.

"The Roy G Biv's seemed to think it was mostly the way it happened," Mr. Tinker replied.

"And what about this Nome you're looking for? The one who took your Lunar Gems?" Aadon continued on. "I've never seen a Nome before since I've only been in Oz about ten years or so, but I've heard tell of them and how they all seem to have gone away over the last hundred years."

"All but one, the way this Nome tells it," Mr. Tinker said, recalling his conversation with Kaliko as he repaired Enarc Brenkert.

Aadon Blu stood up and looked out the nearby window at the eastern horizon with the setting sun just touching it.

"Well, it's late and you could surely use some rest. Besides, I could use the company, what with Boris off visiting family in the Dark Forest of the North," Aadon said. "And he won't be back for some time."

"Thank you," Mr. Tinker said gratefully. "It's been a couple of days since I've had any sleep... Did you say he's visiting family in the Dark Forest?"

"Yes," Aadon replied.

"That's an odd place to live," Mr. Tinker suggested.

"Not if you're a spider... and a rather large one like Boris is," Aadon said matter-of-factly.

Mr. Tinker swallowed hard and tried to smile. He had a fear of spiders for as long as he could remember and was very glad Boris was not at home.

"You can sleep in Boris's nest if you like, but I'm willing to bet you'd prefer the couch?" Aadon chuckled as he pointed to a large silken nest in the far corner of the living room.

Mr. Tinker nodded his head in agreement. A spider's nest was no place he ever wanted to fall asleep in.

Within the hour, both were fast asleep as the full moon passed over the little house by the Pinwheel Fields.

Chapter 28
The Meeting Of The
Dragonflies & Damselflies

The Herd of Dragonflies gathered around on the lily pads that had just grown back up from where the Dragonettes had eaten them the day before. Though they weren't fully grown, the lily pads were strong enough for the Dragonflies to hold their meeting.

Nearby, the Damselflies were also meeting among the nearly half grown cattails near the Singular Oak.

All of Lake Nogard was buzzing with excitement as their wings made a large humming noise that rose all the way up to Nogard Castle, where Drago was playing with many of the local children from the nearby village.

For many, the frequent destruction of their kingdom was the only thing on their minds, but for most, the Exodus of the Nomes was their main concern.

It seems that Dragonflies and Damselflies have a unique insight into the world around them; and for them, the Exodus of the Nomes caused them to be very concerned. They understood that when a Nome chose to leave the Dominion of the Nomes, they took with them a little bit of the magic that makes the Fairy Lands surrounding Oz, as well as the Land of Oz itself special.

"If we don't find a way to convince the Nomes to return, I fear that the magic they take with them will never return," Odon explained to his comrades on the lily pads.

"And if that happens, Princess Ozma may lose Her power, and if that happens, the Land of Oz, our home, will vanish forever… never to return," Anis explained to her comrades among the cattails.

Suddenly, the buzzing of excitement took an ominous tone and even Drago, far up the hill by Castle Nogard, could tell that something was not right with the citizens of Lake Nogard.

"I found another one and tried to get his attention," Speedo informed Odon, "but he just stood there and didn't say a word. I even saw his fishing pole bob up and down, and yet he didn't say a word or even move a muscle."

There was a buzz of excitement as Speedo told his tale.

"Even the other Nome across the street was watching us too and he never said a word either," Speedo continued as his wings dipped down in defeat.

"That's hard to believe!" exclaimed Snail, a comrade of Speedo with bright silver wings and jet black body.

"Well, it's true!" replied Speedo as he looked around at his fellow Dragonflies.

"What's wrong with everyone these days?" Speedo asked as he looked around.

"Everyone is caught up in their own world, that's what is happening," Snail said as he shook his head and wings furiously.

"So what are we going to do?" Flash asked. "There has got to be a way to talk to them and explain to them that they have to return to our world."

"We have got to come up with a plan. There just has to be a way to get through to them," Speedo replied.

Just then, the large gathering of Damselflies flew over from their gathering place to join the Dragonflies.

They were led by Anis, and like the Dragonflies, they too had come to the conclusion that something had to be done to convince the Nomes to return to the Land of Oz and the Dominion of the Nomes.

She conferred with her brother Odon while the other Dragonflies and Damselflies made a great noise and flew about.

"Listen up everyone!" Odon shouted loudly above the noise. "Listen up!! We need quiet!!!"

Word quickly passed among the gathering and soon, the humming and buzzing of wings came to a halt.

"Now, we need to get word out to every gnome we can find, so go far and wide to every gnome we know of. Don't stop until you find every last one of them. It's very important!" Odon explained sternly.

Just then, an odd sensation passed over the gathering and everyone quickly realized that a Nome had appeared from an odd tunnel that showed up near Drago's home.

Odon sent Speedo up to check out the mountainside near Nogard Castle where Drago was standing, face to face with the new Nome.

A few minutes later, Speedo came rushing back with news of the new Nome.

Chapter 29
Kaliko's Ride

Heavenlee watched, along with the other children, as Kaliko prodded Drago and urged him forward and to the west, where he knew the Land of Oogaboo lay.

There was a great sadness and many of the children cried as Drago and his Master vanished over the far hill to the west. They all ran home to their parents, including Heavenlee, who was the last to leave the grounds of Castle Nogard. It was her sad duty to tell Dragonelli that her mate, father to her Dragonettes, had been "stolen by a Nome named Kaliko."

Fortunately for the handful of Dragonflies who were sent by Odon and Anis to observe, Drago seemed to be taking a land route rather than go airborne. Both Speedo and Snail were glad for this, certain that an airborne Dragon would be very hard to keep up with.

As for Kaliko, he kept a steady pace for Drago, who plodded along unwillingly, but unable to stop.

The old Nome had decided not to go airborne as he had always preferred to stay grounded to the soil during his younger days of riding Dragons. He was however, uncertain as to how long it would take to get to Oogaboo since he had no idea how far he was from it. The Dragon upon which he sat seemed in no mood to offer his opinion and Kaliko preferred the silence of the beast.

The vast purple landscape of Gillikin Country passed slowly by as Kaliko and Drago made their way westward towards Oogaboo. There was an occasional small stream or creek to cross and Drago did require a stop at each for water and some vegetation for food.

Kaliko never dismounted the Dragon, preferring to remain astride of Drago and maintain his control. The pouch of Lunar Gems glowed brightly as he uttered his commands of left or right, stop or go.

For two full days and nights, they plodded silently along, meeting an occasional citizen of the northern Gillikin Country who would offer Kaliko food and water, most of which Kaliko refused.

At one point, they even passed a large field of pinwheels, which Drago had stopped momentarily at to see if they smelled pretty or not.

Kaliko dug his heels in and commanded the Dragon to "move on!" at the sight of strangers on the horizon.

The power of the Lunar Gems had begun to affect his reason, and soon paranoia took hold of the former Chief Steward to Ruggedo.

Chapter 30
Zoe

The gnome with the fishing pole stood at his post, rock hard of course, for he couldn't move any more today than he could yesterday, or the years before that.

The neighborhood girls were all playing in the yard and he could hear their shrill screaming and yelling.

"If ever I could get a headache, today would be the day," he thought to himself.

Suddenly, one of the older girls began yelling a name.

"Zoe!" she shouted for the whole neighborhood to hear.

Soon, some of the other girls began shouting.

"Zo-ee! Zo-ee! Zo-ee!" they chanted, dancing about the yard as they did so.

"Where is she?" one of the girls asked.

"I don't know. She was just here a few minutes ago," another girl replied.

The fishing gnome stood there, alone now after the pink flamingos had flown south during a wild storm one night.

The name Zoe kept echoing in his mind.

"Why does that name sound familiar?" thought the gnome to himself. *"Zo-ee. Where have I heard that name before? Hmmm... Z...O...E. I know I've heard that, or something like it before."*

"Ah, there she is!" shouted the oldest girl.

The word 'Ah" floated around the fishing gnome's head, though only he could see it, for he seemed suddenly lost in thought.

"*Ah... Zoe... Ah... Zo... Hmmm... Ah..Z... Ahz...*"

Suddenly, out of nowhere came a flying softball that bounced neatly off the side of the fishing gnome's head, coming to rest near where the pink flamingos used to stand.

"You win!!!" shouted one of the girls.

The fishing gnome suddenly felt a wave of revelation as the word 'OZ' washed over him like a returning memory.

Just as quickly as it came to him, it went away, leaving the fishing gnome alone and speechless, as usual.

Across the street, the gnome holding the staff watched on, grateful that the girls weren't throwing objects at him.

Chapter 31
The Near Miss

The following morning found Aadon Blu and his guest up at dawn and enjoying a great breakfast of cornmeal pudding and toast, along with some fruit juice.

"I trust the couch was to your liking?" Aadon inquired.

Mr. Tinker stretched and yawned and was generally pleased with the accommodations.

"Yes… and your cooking was fabulous," the little tinker from Ev complimented. He was very pleased by the all food he had missed while away on the Moon.

Mr. Tinker and Aadon Blu discussed the dilemma regarding the Lunar Gems and it was decided to head east towards the far reaches of Gillikin Country, in the Eastern Peaks.

Aadon had spoken with numerous people over the five or so years he had spent in service to the former Wizard of Oz as Caretaker of the Pinwheel Fields.

Now, with young Jamie Diggs, great grandson of the old Wizard of Oz in charge of the duties handed down by Princess Ozma, the Pinwheel Fields saw an increase in potential visitors as everyone wanted to meet the new Royal Magician of Oz.

In all, he had heard of at least a dozen different Nomes that had found escape from Oz in the east, beyond the Eastern Peaks.

Mr. Tinker had only his haversack and was ready to begin his search for Kaliko almost immediately.

For Aadon Blu, it would take an hour to gather what he felt was needed and he still had questions.

"Who said you were going with me?" Mr. Tinker asked Aadon Blu, who was approaching with a full pack and an umbrella as a walking stick.

"If you've been gone as long as you say you have, you've missed all the fun... and Oz is nothing like you remember," Aadon informed his guest. "Besides, you have no clue where you want to go, do you?"

Mr. Tinker thought for a moment, his brow furrowing as he plunged into deep thought.

"Before you answer, let me suggest this," Aadon said slyly as he wrapped his arm around the tinker shoulders. "You could use some help... and I see an opportunity to chase an adventure, which doesn't happen very often in a field full of pinwheels."

Mr. Tinker couldn't argue with Aadon Blu's logic and accepted his fate. Besides, he was growing to like the company of others and the joy of conversation and such. After a hundred years in isolation upon the Moon, the warmth of friendship and fellowship, as well as camaraderie, was keenly felt by the little tinker from Ev.

As they stepped out onto the porch of the little house that stood entryway into the Pinwheel Fields, a fresh breeze lifted their spirits even more that they already were. The rising sun in the west bathed them in warming sunlight as Aadon Blu and Mr. Tinker set out to find the Lunar Gems.

For nearly half a day, Mr. Tinker and Aadon Blu made steady progress eastward towards the Eastern Peaks, stopping here and there for rest and refreshment. The few locals they encountered offered food and such freely, as is the custom in Oz for most folk who live there, although there are a few who prefer solitude and isolation.

Fortunately for Mr. Tinker and Aadon Blu, those folks were few and far between.

Instead, they found kind and loving farmers, tradesmen and everyday people, all of whom showered them with friendship and Love.

At one point early in their journey, Aadon pointed towards the southern horizon.

"Look at that," he said with a puzzled look on his face.

Mr. Tinker squinted at the small hulking shape lumbering across the far ridge many miles away.

"That looks like a Dragon, if I'm not mistaken," Aadon suggested.

"Seen many Dragons these days?" Mr. Tinker replied.

Aadon blushed a bit, then chuckled at his new friend.

"To be honest… No." he confessed. "They are supposed to come out only once every hundred years, but if we can see that thing from this far away, it must be huge… and only Dragons are that big, so I'm told."

Once again, Aadon Blu's logic was hard to argue against, and so they decided to keep clear of the massive beast.

As the lumbering hulk passed beyond the horizon towards the west and the Pinwheel Fields, Mr. Tinker felt an odd tingling in his mind. He couldn't quite grasp it enough to examine what it might mean. He only knew that something felt different.

Chapter 32
Bookopolis

After a few hours of walking through the Gillikin countryside, Mr. Tinker and Aadon Blu turned to look southward towards the ever-present green glow of the Emerald City, low on the horizon and inviting for all who see it to come and be joyous.

"Is that the Emerald City?" he asked Aadon, remembering what Joe Merchant had said.

"Yes it is. That's where Princess Ozma rules over all in Oz and where Princess Dorothy lives with her aunt and uncle... and Toto too!" Aadon exclaimed.

Mr. Tinker decided to ask his new friend and traveling companion the one question he had forgotten to ask the night before.

"How did you come to Oz?" he inquired.

Aadon Blu furrowed his brow ever so slightly and looked about for a spot to stop, rest and speak of his Redemption from Death. He pointed to a nearby creek with a Weeping Willow Tree dipping its branches into the slowly flowing blue waters and providing a spot of shade and calm.

"It is Princess Ozma who tells me of this, for I have no memory of my Life before arriving here in Oz nearly ten years ago."

Aadon spoke somberly as the two friends sat down by the clear blue waters and partook of some provisions that Aadon had thoughtfully brought along from home.

"Do go on, my friend," Mr. Tinker implored.

Aadon finished his thought and returned to his arrival in Oz.

"It would seem that I was a child, beset by Evil and sent to Death, only to be called back by Her Majesty, Princess Ozma in what She called an Act of Redemption," Aadon said slowly. "My soul must have cried out for help... for She answered it and brought me here."

Mr. Tinker remained silent for a time, with only the sounds of the water gurgling by and an occasional Dragonfly buzzing the flora and fauna of the creek.

When they resumed their way eastward, they soon found themselves surrounded by a vast field of purple blooming clover. The sweet smell was nearly enough to put one to sleep... almost enough, at least.

"What's that?" Mr. Tinker said, pointing towards an object laying among the purple buds of the clover.

151

When they were standing directly above it, Aadon nodded his head in recognition. He had seen this thing before.

"It's the Bookites and their village, Bookopolis," Aadon said as he pointed at the lone book among the clover. On the cover was the title:

Bookopolis

"Their sayings make no sense to me… but maybe they will to you?" Aadon suggested.

He reached down and slowly peeled back the front cover. The cover grew larger and larger as it grew in overall size until it nearly covered the hillside.

There, in paper, was the title page, 50 feet wide and 50 feet long, and on it read the title:

The Facts of Oz

by

The Bookites

Edited by the Ozsnobs

Published by

Scientia Est Vox Press

"Go ahead and flip the page," Aadon invited. He knew from experience that the paper was as light as air, and yet un-rippable.

Mr. Tinker grabbed the nearby corner of the immensely huge sheet of paper and found it to be *as light as air,*" he thought to himself.

As the tile page landed gently on its backside, the open book now revealed a series of small books, each one roughly five feet square and spread about, much like a small village.

Mr. Tinker counted seven books in all within Bookopolis and noticed to himself that the books were numbered 1 through seven.

"I've opened them once before and it was a very confusing experience," Aadon informed Mr. Tinker.

Mr. Tinker had always loved a challenge, so this came as a welcomed happenstance.

As he opened the first book, it too was light as air and the now open book featured a pop-up house and a small figure, both of whom had doubled in size as the book opened fully.

Mr. Tinker watched as the figure, which was about four feet high or so, walk back and forth, constrained by a nearly invisible wire that attached it to the house, which looked to be about ten feet high and ten feet square. On the front facing above the small porch was the number 1.

Both appeared to be made of paper and were fashioned in a manner Mr. Tinker had once heard referred to as Origami, a style of paper-folding.

The small figure had writing upon its chest and Mr. Tinker read it as the thing marched by him... then read it again on the return march.

Toto was Jerry

Mr. Tinker puzzled over the figure and its message. He recalled how the Roy G Biv's had noticed that the little dog ENARC BRENKERT had shown looked a lot like Toto, who nearly everyone in Oz knew... everyone except him.

He looked at Aadon Blu, who could only shrug his shoulders in response.

The next book, which had the number 2 painted prominently on its front, revealed a similar house and what Aadon Blu confirmed was one of the Bookites mentioned on the title page.

On the chest of the pacing paper figure was printed:

Dorothy's house fell backwards

He remembered seeing the house fall from above when it landed on what the Roy G Biv's were certain was the Wicked Witch of the East.

He moved on to the next book, which opened up to reveal a nearly identical paper pop-up house and marching figure. On the front of the house read the number 3.

Once more, the figure sported writing on his chest, which read:

The Magic Slippers are silver!

Mr. Tinker was now certain these books had some connection to ENARC BRENKERT, though what it was, he had no clue. He did recall clearly how the Roy G Biv's had lamented that the Magic Slippers should have been silver, not rubies.

Aadon just watched silently as Mr. Tinker opened book after book and puzzling over the message from within.

The next book, number 4, was house number 4 and the message:

That's no Munchkin, it's a large bird!

Mr. Tinker was stumped by this one, since the only large birds he could recall were near the house of the Tin Woodman, not in Munchkin City.

The next book, being number 5, was even odder.

The Horse-of-a-Different-Color loved Jell-O

By now, both men were flabbergasted by Bookopolis and what Aadon Blu confirmed were the Facts of Oz.

"There was that horse that changed colors," Mr. Tinker mused out loud.

Aadon remained silent and quite puzzled.

House number 6 was a bit more familiar to Mr. Tinker as he read the Fact of Oz out loud.

Nikko is a Winged Monkey

He remembered the Winged Monkeys from his days just before leaving Oz and setting up shop on the Moon, though he had never met one personally.

The last book Mr. Tinker chose to open was the last book yet unread, with the number 7 prominently displayed and both men were curious how odd the final Fact of Oz would be.

The Dark Side of the Rainbow is real

Mr. Tinker stood there, dumbfounded by the revelation of the 7th Fact of Oz. He thought no one had seen him project his Rainbow on the Dark Side of the Moon, and now, a paper figure, marching about in front of a pop-up paper house, both of which reside in a book within a book, was speaking to him from the shadow region beyond the Lunar North Pole.

Mr. Tinker suddenly realized that Aadon Blu was snapping his fingers in front of him. He shook his head and cleared his thoughts.

"You okay there?" Aadon asked, clearly concerned for his friend. "You went blank for a moment."

Mr. Tinker thought back to that moment where Time seemed to stand still as the Rainbow on the Dark Side of the Moon danced across the darkened surface of the Moon.

Just then, a flash of orange and a feeling of familiarity overtook Mr. Tinker and he soon realized that the Lunar Gems were *"somewhere over by that gathering of peaks, about a half a day's walk from here, "*he thought to himself.

"I feel like we should head over to those small peaks in the distance," Mr. Tinker suggested to Aadon as he pointed to the northeast at the nearby circle of rising rock and stone.

Aadon Blu recognized the area well as he had been just south of there several times.

"Those are the Eastern Peaks," he informed Mr. Tinker. "As I recall, they're home to a family of Dragons, but I've never seen them the few times I visited the area."

The little tinker from Ev nodded his head and studied the five encircling peaks.

Aadon pointed towards the southern-most peak.

"Just south of there is a small village that is the northern-most port-of-call for the Munchkin River. From there, you can get anywhere in Oz the river passes near," Aadon Blu explained. "I've sailed from there a handful of times in search of supplies and items of need, though I've never been farther south than where it crosses the road of yellow brick."

Both men agreed on their next destination and Mr. Tinker went about, closing each book and marveling at the ingenuity of the Origami paper-folding creations known as the Bookites.

As each book would slowly close, the wire attaching the small paper figure to the house would retract slowly as well, drawing the figure back into the book as it closed.

"It was told to me by others who have read Bookopolis that the Bookites never stray far from their book as they fear being left out when it closes. They are happiest when opened, since that means they're being read," Aadon explained as Mr. Tinker closed all but the last book, number 1.

Mr. Tinker stopped the paper figure, who continued marching, but only marching in place rather than back and forth.

The little tinker from Ev poked and prodded about the folds of paper until he was able to determine the inner workings as best he could.

"It has a paper mechanism of sorts... something like the inner workings of a pocket watch or perhaps even like Tik-Tok's mechanics, if I remember right," Mr. Tinker muttered to himself.

"Are they alive?" Aadon asked.

"No, I think not," Mr. Tinker replied. "It's like Tik-Tok, who once told me that he prided himself in his lifelessness."

Moments later and book number 1 was closed tight, as was Bookopolis itself, which promptly shrank in size until it was as small as it had been when the two friends happened upon it earlier.

Aadon Blu and Mr. Tinker turned from Bookopolis and headed due east and slightly north to the circlet of peaks off in the distance, leaving the book lying alone if the vast field of purple clover.

Chapter 33
Pan Fried Morel Mushrooms

It had been several more hours of walking after their encounter with Bookopolis when the two friends decided to make camp for the night. A small stream and yet another Weeping Willow Tree made for an ideal campsite.

Within the hour, Mr. Tinker had provided a small campfire while Aadon Blu sought out some berries and nuts that would go well with the bread and cheese he had brought along for the journey.

Given the generosity of the local folks they had encountered throughout the day, their food supplies had hardly been touched at all.

"I came across some lovely mushrooms near that old log downstream," Aadon said as he held out a handful of what appeared to be Morel Mushrooms.

"Are they safe to eat?" Mr. Tinker inquired cautiously. He had grown mushrooms during his stay at Mare Imbrium from spores he had brought along with him when he first travelled to the Moon and was quite fond of them.

"Of course they are," Aadon assured him. "They're called Morels and these kinda appeared about five years ago after the new Royal Magician of Oz had brought one from his home in the Great Outside.

"They don't look like the ones I grew," Mr. Tinker observed."They look more like an old sponge."

He listened intently as Aadon Blu explained how a great number of the Morel Mushrooms had banded together, having somehow been enchanted, and were dispatched by the Sycamore and his Army of Fighting Trees to take up battle against the Tin Woodman.

"Apparently, the Tin Woodman had chopped up some of the Fighting Trees long ago when he first journeyed with Dorothy towards the Emerald City in search of the Wizard of Oz," Aadon explained. "And they wanted revenge… and somehow, the Marauding Morel Mushrooms, as they came to be known, were enlisted to help."

By now, Mr. Tinker had sliced up some bread to go with the nuts, berries and mushrooms. He sliced up the Morel Mushrooms and placed them into a cast iron skillet Aadon Blu had brought along. They sizzled as they landed in the melted butter he had dropped in moments before, which a local farmer had given them earlier that day. He had also picked a few limes from a nearby lime tree and squeezed the juice into two wooden cups full of water for refreshment.

A few minutes later and dinner was served as the smell of the fried Morel Mushrooms wafted across the landscape.

Aadon continued his story in between mouthfuls of dinner.

"It was the new Royal Magician of Oz who used his magic to defeat the Army of Fighting Trees, but it was Dorothy who had cast her first spell ever and transformed the entire Army of Marauding Morel Mushrooms into stone," he said dramatically.

Mr. Tinker gasped slightly.

"Somehow though, spores shed off by those very mushrooms have made their way across Oz and now we can enjoy them in all their tasty goodness," Aadon said as he popped a final fried Morel Mushroom into his mouth and ate if gleefully.

The evening soon found Aadon Blu and Mr. Tinker fast asleep on a carpet of soft purple moss beneath the Weeping Willow Tree.

The next morning, Aadon and Mr. Tinker were up at dawn and soon heading once more towards the Eastern Peaks, which were much closer now than when they had started.

By mid-morning, Aadon Blu noticed something and stopped to take a listen.

"Can you hear that sound?" he asked.

Mr. Tinker heard only the sound of a gentle breeze rushing through the purple field grass and he shook his head.

Aadon seemed certain he had heard something, but decided he had been mistaken and the two friends continued on.

Within the hour, Mr. Tinker stopped and listened carefully.

"Is that what you heard earlier?" he asked.

Softly, as though from a great distance away came a sad, mournful sound, as though someone was crying.

"That sounds very sad," Aadon observed.

They continued on as the Eastern Peaks grew closer and closer.

By noon, the soft sound was now much louder and was more of a wailing sound that seemed to echo across the fields.

"It seems to be coming from the Eastern Peaks," Aadon said as he cocked his ear towards the five encircling peaks, now nearly upon them.

Mr. Tinker agreed.

"I can't stand to see, or hear someone cry," Aadon said sadly. "We should see if we can offer any help or comfort to whomever is making that sad sound."

Once again, Mr. Tinker agreed and the two of them made their way along a path that led into a small valley between two of the Eastern Peaks.

As they did, the wailing sound grew louder and Mr. Tinker could tell that it was actually more than one crying and wailing, especially since with each wailing sound, the ground shook gently beneath their feet.

Within an hour, Mr. Tinker and Aadon Blu came upon the very sound that had drawn them into the circle of peaks and were confronted by the sight of a large Dragon and six smaller Dragons, each one crying without pause next to what looked like a large castle of stone.

Even more unsettling to the two were what appeared to be a mother and daughter standing next to the crying Dragons, trying to console them, without much success.

Chapter 34
Dragon's Tears

Dragonelli and her six Dragonettes were crying loud and long, wailing as only Dragons and Dragonettes can do and shaking the ground in the process. The stones in the nearby Nogard Castle shook gently with each wailing moan and rush of tears.

For the family of Dragons, the loss of Drago was as sharp as their very teeth, and equally full of despair. There had never been a time when the family had been parted… and now, Drago was lumbering across the Gillikin countryside of Oz, somehow under the control of Nome who appeared out of nowhere, as they usually do.

Nearby, taking refuge in the immense front hallway of Nogard Castle was Heavenlee and her mother, Darlene. They had remained behind to offer any help they could, having no fear of Dragons nor Dragonettes.

"Remember Heavenlee, we endured the Shadow Demon and Cobbler the Dog, so what's a couple of Dragons to us?" Darlene had asked her daughter when Dragonelli and her Dragonettes first learned from Heavenlee of Drago's enchantment. She was trying her best not to let her daughter see the slight twinge of fear that comes with facing a Dragon, *"even if I am here to offer any help I can,"* Darlene had thought to herself.

Now, it's one thing to suggest offering help to a mother Dragon and her six Dragonette Daughters; it's quite another to actually do it… and Darlene was finding it difficult to remain calm in the face of seven wailing, moaning, crying and otherwise miserable Dragon and Dragonettes.

Heavenlee, on the other hand, was eager to jump in and speak to the Dragonettes, who she felt a kinship with.

After all, Heavenlee and the Dragonettes were all just daughters under their mother's scrutiny.

"Come on, Mom!" Heavenlee pleaded. "Look how sad they are. There has to be something we can do to help."

The look in her eye told Darlene that 'no' was not an option, so she took her daughter by the hand and the two of them consoled Dragonelli as best they could, while gaining strength and confidence from each other's valor.

The Dragonettes however, were nearly inconsolable with the enchantment and enslavement of their father. Drago had been the foundation of the family, and now that foundation was gone. For them, there was no consoling.

Darlene and Heavenlee soon discovered that consoling Dragons was a lot harder than they it would be.

Dragonelli shed tears that would fill a bucket to the brim, and more than once, both Heavenlee and her mother found themselves soaked to the skin in Dragonelli's tears.

Chapter 35
Mother, Daughter & Damselfly

Anis, Leader of the Damselflies had decided rather quickly that the mother and daughter possessed an Aura of Goodness, not to mention a fresh layer of Dragon's Tears, which made them trustworthy and kind and therefore worth meeting. So it began that the Damselflies approached the mother and daughter and made signs of peace and Love.

Darlene and her daughter, Heavenlee likewise felt a kinship with the Damselflies that had greeted them upon their arrival.

"They're so beautiful," Heavenlee had exclaimed. Her mother heartedly agreed.

"And what's more," Darlene explained, "these lovely insects feel so kind and full of Goodness. I'm certain of that."

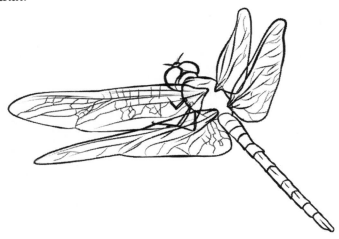

With that, both forces joined together in a futile attempt at consoling the distraught Dragon and Dragonettes.

Sadly for the Damselflies, they too discovered the futility of trying to console weeping, wailing Dragon and Dragonettes.

The more Heavenlee, Darlene, Anis and the nearly a thousand Damselflies tried their best to console the distraught family of Dragons, the more things became inconsolable, especially for the Dragonettes.

Finally, Dragonelli managed to bring her emotions under control enough to speak with the little girl who had brought such devastating news to her and her Dragonettes.

"We just want Drago back home," Dragonelli said between soft sobs of anguish.

The Dragonettes also found their composure and in between their own soft sobs, expressed their desire for their father to be returned to them.

It was a full day and then some when Speedo, reporting in from his surveillance of Drago and the Nome to Anis had alerted Heavenlee and her mother of the presence of strangers approaching from the west.

"It's the Caretaker of the Pinwheel Fields and a stranger, known to none of us," Speedo reported in a calm yet measured voice. He had come across Aadon Blu numerous times before during his patrols of the Gillikin countryside and everyone in Gillikin Country knew about the Pinwheel Fields. "They are nearly upon us, my lady."

No sooner had Speedo completed his report to Anis when the approach of strangers caused a commotion

among the throngs of Damselflies gathered about near
Nogard Castle.

Chapter 36
Heavenlee And Aadon Meet

The Dragonettes, sensing the approach of strangers, retreated into the inner confines of their Nursery, content to wait out the new arrivals. They had no desire for strangers to see them sad. Theirs was a private anguish, not for the eyes and ears of outsiders. Their mother would protect them from all harm.

"There, look!" Heavenlee exclaimed. She pointed westward towards the narrow pass that gained entrance to the circlet of peaks. It was one of several ways to enter the realm of Nogard Lake and Castle.

Darlene instinctively reached out and embraced Heavenlee, surrounding her with loving and protecting arms.

Approaching Castle Nogard at a leisurely pace was a young man in his early twenties, or so he appeared; and an older gentlemen in clothing from an earlier era of Oz. Both seemed glad the wailing and moaning had subsided upon their arrival.

"Greetings!" shouted Mr. Tinker, who suddenly realized that he was shouting over the silence.

Aadon Blu just shook his head and rolled his eyes.

"Greetings," Aadon Blu said in a much more welcoming tone and manner. "We couldn't help but notice the sad emotions pouring forth from this place as we passed by."

Mr. Tinker snorted ever so slightly.

"The whole countryside couldn't help but notice," Mr. Tinker observed.

Aadon elbowed the little tinker from Ev right in the ribcage, which caused a slight "hmph" from Mr. Tinker.

Darlene chuckled a bit, as did her daughter and more than a few of the Damselflies who were buzzing about.

"Your friend is right," Darlene said with a grin.

"My name is Aadon Blu. I am the Caretaker of the Pinwheel Fields due west of here… and this is my friend, Mr. Tinker, who's been away a while," Aadon Blu said.

"And my name is Darlene… and this is my daughter, Heavenlee," Darlene replied. Everyone shook hands and smiled.

Aadon looked at the little girl, sensing some familiarity about her.

"Are you the Heavenlee that the Royal Magician of Oz once told me about?" Aadon inquired of Heavenlee.

Heavenlee blushed and nodded in agreement. No matter how many times Heavenlee was recognized for her role in defeating the Shadow Demon of Oz and her presence at the Battle of Cobbler the Dog, she still felt some slight embarrassment because people wanted to call her 'hero'; and all she did was *help save a friend,* she would tell herself.

For the next half hour or so, Heavenlee and her mother recounted the stories of the Royal Magician of Oz's defeat of the Shadow Demon, and how Heavenlee had help save her new friend, Buddy from certain doom. She blushed slightly whenever she spoke about Buddy and Aadon felt certain Heavenlee must have had a crush on Buddy.

Darlene spoke about Cobbler the Dog, who had been enchanted by the Spirit of the Wicked Witch of the East and made to roam the land, setting the fields and farmhouses of Oz on fire.

Heavenlee spoke of how the Royal Magician of Oz, alongside the Queen of the Field Mice and Her subjects, defeated the mechanical wonder that served as a pet for Tik-Tok; The Army of Oz.

Aadon thoroughly enjoyed Darlene and Heavenlee's account of what had happened, since he knew only what Jamie Diggs, the Royal Magician of Oz had told him... and it was clear Jamie Diggs was far more brave and resourceful than he let on. Aadon would have to tease him about it the next time they met up.

Heavenlee then explained to Mr. Tinker and Aadon Blu about the capture and enchantment of Drago by a Nome who appeared from nowhere when a hole opened up in a nearby mountainside of stone.

Mr. Tinker recognized the Nome Heavenlee had described immediately. It was Kaliko and he was on the right trail but going in the wrong direction.

"I wonder if that lumbering Dragon we saw yesterday was this one?" he asked himself. He recalled the familiar feeling he had felt as it had lumbered off beyond the horizon.

Meanwhile, Dragonelli watched as the people below her talked to each other and totally forgot that she was there.

"Ahem!" Dragonelli coughed loudly as a small burst of bright orange flame shot out of her nostrils and straight up in the air.

Both Darlene and Heavenlee emitted a small shriek at the suddenness of Dragonelli's reminder about her presence.

Mr. Tinker and Aadon Blu uttered muffled gasps at their first confrontation with a Dragon.

"It's okay," Heavenlee said reassuringly. "We are all friends here."

Her words seemed to calm everyone down, especially Dragonelli, who was doing everything she could not to lose control and begin sobbing uncontrollably once more.

"Can you describe what you saw happen when the Nome took control of Drago?" Mr. Tinker asked Heavenlee.

Heavenlee pursed her lips and thought for a moment or two.

"The Nome spoke to Drago in a very strange way… almost like he was controlling him," she replied. "Drago couldn't do anything to resist. His eyes were blank."

172

Dragonelli let out a long wail of sobbing as tears rained down on the four people below.

It took another five minutes before Dragonelli could control herself enough for Heavenlee to finish explaining what had happened.

"And every time he spoke, this white pouch on his belt would glow," Heavenlee recounted, almost as an after-thought.

That last statement caught both the attention of Mr. Tinker; as well as Anis, who had been buzzing about, landing here and there, and all the while listening in on the conversations of the people with Dragonelli.

Chapter 37
Scouting Reports

Anis flew back to her Herd of Damselflies, who were gathered together with the Herd of Dragonflies and Odon, their leader near the Singular Oak, among the newly grown lily pads and cattails.

"The Nome is carrying what I believe to be a satchel of magical gems," she informed her brother, Odon.

He flew around in circles for a short time, pondering the predicament that had plagued them alongside of Dragonelli and her Dragonettes.

Anis joined her brother in flight and the two of them spoke back and forth while circling each other and racing about the stems and reeds that circled the Singular Oak.

"If they are indeed magical gems, then we should be able to transport some of that magic to our wayward Nomes," Anis advised her brother.

"And that should help them return to Oz," Odon advised back.

"If they want to, that is," Anis said as brother and sister circled each other in ever-shrinking arcs until their wings were grazing against each others.

"They must!" Odon declared as the two broke apart and headed for the Herds.

By the time, Anis had joined her sister Damselflies, Odon was already gathering reports from his brother Dragonflies who had been sent out to observe and report back on the whereabouts and the whyfors of Drago and the Nome.

Soon, more scouts were reporting back that Drago and his captor were past the Pinwheel Fields and beyond the borders of Gillikin Country, having passed through the massive valley that separates the Dark Forest of Gillikin Country and the Great Northern Mountain range where O.Z. Diggs, the former Wizard of Oz and his family live.

Chapter 38
Gnome-ly Visions

Gnorm the Gnome watched the green Dragonfly as it flew around his head. He tried shouting at the creature, but to no avail. Although he could talk to himself, which he did often, he had been unable to move any part of his stone body. That included his mouth, which remained frozen in a permanent smile.

Standing silently, the little stone garden gnome felt the light touch of the green Dragonfly as it landed softly upon his outstretched, yet immovable hand.

He glanced across the yard to where the little girl who lived there, along with two girls from the farmhouse up the road, were playing with a large wooden doll house.

It was painted in various shades of green, with trim and accents in various colors of red, blue, yellow, purple and green.

Suddenly, a vision passed through the little stone gnome and flashes of strange lands and even stranger creatures coursed through his mind.

Visions of emeralds, rubies, diamonds and sapphires danced about his inner-eye and Gnorm the Gnome longed to discover what his vision meant.

He had been in the yard of the old Hoosier farmhouse for as long as he could recall and the little garden gnome knew there had to be more than just the house and the yard and road passing by. He was certain wondrous things lay beyond the Tree-In-The-Road, by the cemetery down the road from him.

As the young girls played with the doll house and a number of their own dolls as well, their joyous laughter filled Gnorm with a kind of sadness that comes from being apart from other creatures like himself.

He longed to be among his own kind, whatever that may be, and to be able to move about; not standing still and silent in one place for all time… and he despised being rained upon.

Just then, several neighborhood boys, all roughly the same age, came crashing through the yard of the little garden gnome across the street from Ruggedo. They had fashioned make-shift swords and were making great fun from their imaginary battles.

The gnome stood firm, ready to brandish the stout wooden staff he held in his left hand, but knowing very well that all he could do was watch the boys *"having all the fun,"* he thought to himself.

The small copper-colored Dragonfly buzzed in behind the pointed cap of the little garden gnome and landed up against it.

Just then, a flash of a past memory, hidden away for so long, burst forth.

Visions of fighting and yelling and the camaraderie of battle flooded the staff-wielding gnome's mind and he found himself reveling in it.

Revelations of war and conquest overwhelmed the little garden gnome… and yet he fought back and made himself master of those visions, all while remaining solid as a rock… and just as silent.

Chapter 39
The Offer Of The Dragonflies

It had been Heavenlee who had watched Drago leave with Kaliko the Nome and it was she who had told Dragonelli and the Dragonettes the sad news about Drago.

Recalling the story for Mr. Tinker made her ponder and think about what the Nome had done to have the influence over Drago and to *"get him to leave like that"*, she had thought to herself.

Heavenlee had only met Drago a few weeks before when her mother and her had chartered a small boat for a journey of exploration up the Munchkin River. Each had never been farther north than the road of yellow brick and both were having great fun... up until now, that is.

She knew under no other circumstances would Drago have left the children like he did. She was amazed at how protective a Dragon could be, even one as kind and gentle as Drago. It was his actions that had protected them from the Nome who called himself Kaliko... and it was Heavenlee who had stood up to the Nome, only to discover he was hard as stone and just as immovable.

Heavenlee knew in her heart that Drago didn't want to go with the Nome and that he was uncertain and perhaps even afraid of the Nome.

She had seen the small pouch that he had secured to his belt and wondered if perhaps it had something to do with it.

Heavenlee watched a few Dragonflies flying about. She had seen them a few times before Drago left, and now there were quite a few more after his departure. She thought about the stories Drago told them about how magical Dragonflies and Damselflies were.

Just then, she thought she heard a Dragonfly speaking. She looked down at the beautiful iridescent blue wings of a rather large Dragonfly and smiled.

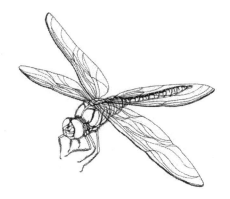

Heavenlee thought to herself, *"How can I understand what a Dragonfly is saying? Dragonflies can't talk to people, can they?"*

The Dragonfly thought he saw the young girl look at him strangely when he spoke to her, asking for her help. The other people, and even the Dragon, didn't even notice that the Dragonfly was talking to them.

Odon spoke once more, imploring the little girl to help them.

"Can you please help us?" he asked.

She looked down at Odon and said, "What can I do to help?"

"Please, we know that the Nome who captured Drago is looking for his fellow Nomes, all of whom have travelled far beyond Oz and into the Great Outside," Odon said somberly. "We know where the other Nomes have gone. We have visited them, but they have been turned to stone and cannot speak to us."

"Can you understand them?" Darlene asked her daughter. It would seem that Darlene, Aadon, Mr. Tinker and even Dragonelli were unable to understand the Dragonflies or Damselflies that were flying about in greater and greater numbers.

"Yes, I can. Can't you?" Heavenlee replied. No one else there could understand the Dragonfly.

For the next half an hour or so, Odon pleaded his case, explaining to Heavenlee, who in turn explained to everyone else, about how the Nomes have been leaving Oz for many years; each one escaping into the Great Outside, only to turn into odd-looking creatures of stone, many of them holding fishing poles and lanterns.

"We are certain that the Nome who took the Dragon with him is the last Nome in Oz; and if he should ever leave Oz in search of his kin, none of them would ever be allowed to return to Oz... ever!" Odon exclaimed.

Once Heavenlee informed the others of the plight of the Nomes, they all agreed that something should be done to help the ever-growing Herd of Dragonflies and Damselflies.

Everyone that is, except Dragonelli, who couldn't understand why banishing all Nomes from the Land of Oz was a bad thing.

"That creature enchanted my mate and is riding him across the countryside, looking for other Nomes!" the distraught Dragon declared. "I say let the Nomes be gone from here forever!"

The Dragonflies and Damselflies could tell that the Dragon was not interested in helping them, even if they couldn't understand her language.

Mr. Tinker cleared his throat and spoke up.

"I remember long ago when Mr. Smith and I had our shop in Ev and King Pastoria had dropped by for a visit. He had spoken of the Nomes in the nearby Dominion of the Nomes and how they were as much a part of Oz and the enchanted lands surrounding it as the very rock and soil and water and air around us. He called them enchanted creatures and lamented that without them, the Land of Oz would lose much of its magical power," he explained.

Heavenlee explained Mr. Tinker's story to Odon, who heartedly agreed with what the little tinker from Ev was saying.

"We must help them stop the Nomes from leaving Oz forever," Aadon said proudly. "To sit back and do nothing would bring sadness and regret to our Land of Oz… and we are better than that."

"But what about Drago?" Dragonelli demanded.

As Heavenlee explained the Dragon's response to Odon, a buzz of curiosity coursed through the Herds of Dragonflies and Damselflies.

"His name is Drago?" Anis said with great curiosity.

"Yes, he is my friend and his name is Drago the Dragon," Heavenlee said proudly.

Another buzz ran through the throngs of Dragonflies and Damselflies as everyone soon learned of the name of the Dragon whose daughters had so ravaged their homes and playgrounds.

"We've never known his name before since we've never been able to ask him" Odon informed Heavenlee.

"Well, this one up there," Heavenlee said as she pointed up at the towering figure of Dragonelli hovering over them, "is named Dragonelli... and Drago is her mate."

"And the other smaller ones are their children?" Anis inquired.

Heavenlee nodded her head as Odon and Anis met in hushed whispers and a buzzing of wings.

Odon turned from Anis and addressed the little girl.

"We know of a way to help you get Drago back, and keep the last Nome in Oz, as well as maybe even getting all the others Nomes to return as well," Odon said slowly and methodically. "But our help comes at a price."

Chapter 40
Jamie Spies A Nome

"You're not looking at gnome again, are you?" Jamie's mother asked the young boy who was looking through the Magic Telescope at the gnome with the pipe.

She knew full well that that Jamie was looking at the garden gnome that now lived at their old home back in Indiana in the Great Outside.

"Think of the future, my boy, not about the past," James chimed in as he passed through on his way to the kitchen for a 'snackipoo', as he called it.

"I was just looking for any Nomes around here," Jamie replied. He backed away from the eyepiece, replaced the clear crystal lens with a yellow crystal lens and swung the brass tube around. It spun for a moment or two, then came to rest, pointing towards the southwest, towards Winkie Country.

"I thought you were looking at gnome," Amanda replied.

"No, I was looking for Nomes, not at gnome… and I can't seem to find any Nomes… just gnome," he lamented.

The young Royal Magician of Oz looked through the eyepiece and saw a sight he had never thought to see in his entire life.

In the small circular view into Winkie Country, Jamie Diggs saw what could only be described as a Nome riding a lumbering Dragon across the yellow countryside, approaching a large river.

He backed away, then had another look at the odd sight in the eyepiece of the Magic Telescope.

"Hey great grandpa!" he yelled to the old man sitting down in the old leather chair at the end of the foyer. "Is this a Nome?"

The old man got up and made his way across the expanse of floor until he was nearly upon the young man and the Magic Telescope.

"Let me have a look at that," exclaimed the former Wizard of Oz. he leaned down and gazed into the brass eyepiece, humming to himself as he did.

"I do believe you are correct, my boy!" he said proudly. "And I do believe it's riding a Dragon."

Chapter 41
The Price Of Freedom

Odon and Dragonelli argued back and forth for nearly an hour, mostly on matters of how and why while Heavenlee struggled to keep up with the rapid pace that the two had set. Each had wants and needs and Heavenlee did her best to convey those needs between the Dragonfly and the Dragon.

The Dragonflies and Damselflies had indeed hatched up a fairly ingenious plan with which to transfer the power of the Lunar Gems to themselves and then on to the Great Outside where the Gnome of Oz now resided.

"How do you know these are the Nomes we're looking for?" Heavenlee asked on behalf of Dragonelli.

"We can't say why, but we just know which ones are only gnome and which ones are actually Nomes," Odon said through the young girl. "It is a power only we Dragonflies and Damselflies posses, though we know not why."

Dragonelli looked hard at Odon. She was still in anguish over Drago's enchantment, but knew better to keep her composure.

The Dragonflies and Damselflies had been a part of the surroundings for as long as the Dragons had, maybe even a little bit longer, and she had no desire to bring harm to others. She only wanted Drago back.

"How will you get there… and back?" Dragonelli asked through Heavenlee.

"We know the way into the Great Outside, through a Nome tunnel that leads to a waterfall entrance, where numerous Nomes have escaped into their fate," Odon replied.

After a time, Dragonelli came to the question that had been on both of their minds.

"And what of this price you mentioned?" Heavenlee spoke slowly and with determination; for she was as curious as the Dragon towering above them all.

By now, the Dragonettes had mustered up their courage and ventured out into the sunlight and the place where their mother was speaking to an insect and a little girl while several other people stood watching.

They listened in as Heavenlee translated Odon's offer to Dragonelli.

"For nearly a hundred years now, your children have eaten our homes and such. Every few years for a few months at a time, we have to endure losing our homes and our way of Life," Heavenlee spoke with some measure of feeling, which she hoped was how the Dragonfly felt. She certainly felt his anguish as he spoke through her.

Odon flew back and forth in anticipation as Heavenlee spoke her language to the Dragon he now knew as Dragonelli.

Heavenlee turned back to him and gave the Dragonfly a nod.

"The Dragonflies and Damselflies agree to help free Drago the Dragon from the control of the Nome," Odon announced in as official a tone as a Dragonfly can muster. "In turn, Dragonelli agrees that the Dragonettes will no longer eat their homes and playgrounds."

Heavenlee had to catch her breath and sought out a small cup of water from the nearby stream that was fed

186

from a small spring and eventually spilled out into Lake Nogard.

All the other's there joined her as Dragonelli and Odon stared at each other, pondering the Dragonfly's offer.

"That's a small price to pay for Drago's freedom," Dragonelli said to no one in particular. She knew there was plenty of food elsewhere around the circlet of peaks that would satisfy the Dragonettes.

As for the Dragonettes, they had gathered around their mother, staring at the singular Dragonfly that was hovering about, flying in tight little circles. They all agreed with much enthusiasm about their mother's words.

When Heavenlee returned to the place where the Dragon and the Dragonfly had chosen to negotiate, she was feeling refreshed and rejuvenated.

"Ain't it great what a little water will do?" she had asked her mother, who nodded in agreement.

"That cheese that Aadon Blu offered us wasn't bad either," Darlene observed.

Both girls nodded their heads and smiled.

"Have you two decided yet?" Heavenlee asked both Odon and Dragonelli.

The Dragon now towering over the entire gathering was glaring at the Dragonfly, who stood his ground... or patch of air, as the case may be.

"Do you still intend to return all of the Nomes to their former homes?" she asked in a menacing tone.

The Dragonettes chimed in as well with the occasional 'hmph' and snort as they paced about behind their mother.

Heavenlee conveyed the question to Odon, who had but a single word in response.

"Yes," came his sharp reply.

Dragonelli didn't need Heavenlee to translate as she understood fully well what the Dragonfly had meant.

The Dragonettes gave muted whimpers and soft pleads to their mother in hopes that she would agree. They desperately wanted their father back... as did Dragonelli.

Chapter 42
Fresh Paint

The gnome watched as the man came walking out of the garage with the paint brushes and several small buckets of paint.

"Finally!" he thought to himself, "I'm getting a new coat." It had been several years since his last one and he was looking rather faded and weather-worn.

The young girl named Zoe was skipping rope and singing to herself. It was a cute little song he knew he had heard from somewhere before.

"But where?" he asked himself.

Ruggedo tried to remember all that he could about Oz, but he just couldn't remember much at all.

He soon realized that the man had finished painting his new coat and the little garden gnome was very pleased.

Then, the thought of Oz returned to the stone gnome, Ruggedo.

Perhaps it was a town we had lived in?" he thought. *"…or maybe something else."*

He was certain he had been with this family for as long as he could remember; but somehow, he could vaguely sense that something was different from before till now. The thought of it gave him concern, since he had been a very happy gnome, up until now.

"It matters not," he thought to himself. *"I don't want to think of anything that would take me away from my family."*

By now, Zoe had moved on to her friend's yard down the street and Ruggedo suddenly that he was all alone.

"They are the only family I have..." he finished his thought.

Later, as the sun hit high noon and shined down upon the little garden gnome with his fishing pole in a cement pond, the former Nome King began thinking about Oz once more.

"Surely they must love me?" he thought to himself as the family got into the large metal box on wheels and drove away. *"After all, they take care of me, paint me a new coat every few annuals, even treat me as one of their own. The children like to play near me and they always tell me their secrets. "*

The local children did indeed share their inner most thoughts with Ruggedo and the other two gnome in the nearby yards, often times just after sunset and into twilight.

"No... I wouldn't want to live anywhere else or with anyone else. After all, I am the Keeper of Secrets!" the former Nome King exclaimed to himself.

No sooner had he declared himself the Keeper of the Secrets when a wave of memory washed over the little stone fishing gnome.

Visions of eggs being rolled towards him brought about a wave of panic and fear.

Ruggedo thought once more about the children who lived in his neighborhood, especially the ones he called 'family', and a joyous wave of Love washed over him.

"Truly, all one ever needs is Love," Ruggedo thought to himself.

Chapter 43
North Munchkin Pier

Once the Dragonettes had voiced their support for Odon's plan, Dragonelli knew that there was no other choice. She was desperate to have Drago return to her and their children... and the Dragonettes were desperate to have their father back.

Dragonelli and the Dragonettes retreated into the confines of Nogard Castle to await the success or failure of the Plan of the Dragonfly. Dragonelli was very unsure that the Dragonflies and Damselflies would succeed while the Dragonettes were certain of success.

Both Odon and Anis had expressed a desire to head out immediately for the west, eager to complete their plan and save their homes, as well as Drago the Dragon.

"They have bedded down for the night alongside the Winkie River," Snail had reported earlier, moments after he had arrived from his surveillance mission.

The sun was nearing the far eastern horizon and would set in an hour, or so Mr. Tinker thought.

There was a general buzz of excitement among the Herds of Dragonflies and Damselflies and they made preparations to fly west through the night in order to catch up with the wayward Dragon and his captor.

"No, wait," Mr. Tinker spoke up. "The magical gems that Nome is carrying belong to me. I gathered them from the Moon as a gift for King Pastoria's crown... only now he is no longer and I wish to give them to his daughter, Princess Ozma."

Odon thought for a time, whispering to Anis as the conferred.

"I would rather fly in daylight than at night," Anis confessed. "We should be able to get there with everyone together in a day, if they can keep up with us."

Odon agreed and the Herd of Dragonflies and Damselflies spent the few remaining minutes of the sun circling the Singular Oak and racing each other through the cattails and lily pads, which had grown back in a day. They all knew that what they were planning to do could be considered using magic, a thing for which Princess Ozma, Sovereign Ruler of Oz had decreed could be done only by Herself, Glinda; Good Witch of the South and Ruler of Quadling Country, and the former Wizard of Oz, O.Z. Diggs; who had reformed himself from the humbug he had been when he ruled Oz.

Such was the rule until a few years ago, when O.Z. Diggs decided to retire as the first and only Royal Magician of Oz.

His great grandson and protégé, Jamie Diggs was soon tested and became the new Royal Magician of Oz and allowed to perform magic, which he has done admirably since his inception into the Land of Oz.

There was that time though when Dorothy cast her Spell of the Stone Morels," Anis had suggested, hoping to find a means to justify their plan.

Odon buzzed noisily, concerned and cautious about the coming day. He didn't like the idea of breaking a rule, especially a royal one, but he was certain that if Kaliko left Oz, a great calamity befall the ancient fairy lands.

While the other Dragonflies and Damselflies amused themselves, the gathering of new friends made their way out of the eastern Peaks and on to the small town that served as the northern-most port of call on the Munchkin River, about an hour away.

Known as North Munchkin Pier, it was a typical dockside village and home to about a hundred folks, all of whom made their living through trade, commerce and by barter, if possible. For them, their livelihood depended on anything and everything connected to the Munchkin River, along which the town lay.

Mr. Tinker, having a keen eye and an understanding of mechanics, quickly surmised where the important buildings were; that being the blacksmith, construction companies and the dockside businesses, while most of the others scouted out a good place to eat.

Mr. Tinker's mind had been racing since Heavenlee had described the Plan of the Dragonfly. He knew he had to get to where Kaliko was in order to recover his Lunar Gems.

"But how are we going to get there quickly?" he mused out loud.

Chapter 44
The Pinwheel Raft

Aadon Blu, who had remained with Mr. Tinker, pointed out a small raft beached high upon the shoreline of the river.

"That looks big enough to hold us," he suggested.

Mr. Tinker agreed and the two of them made their over to speak to someone nearby who might know something about the raft.

Nearby, Heavenlee found herself swamped by her new friends, whom she had met days before while sitting on the back of Drago the Dragon, listening to his stories and all of them telling their own as well.

"Can you really talk to Dragonflies?" one young girl with curly red hair asked timidly.

"Yes," Heavenlee replied. She blushed slightly, then began telling her friends the Plan of the Dragonfly.

There were numerous 'oohs' and 'ahhs' as Heavenlee described the meeting between Dragonelli and Odon.

Darlene could hear the children nearby as she spoke with several ladies engaged in commerce. Each had a small wagon loaded down by vegetables, fruits and other tasty items. Some had small wood-fired burners that they would cook upon.

She watched as the children scattered about and connected with their families.

Heavenlee came strolling up to her mother, smiling and happy.

"I think we'll have no trouble finding help," she said.

Within a few minutes, throngs of parents came walking up to center of North Munchkin Pier, all eager to help the people their children told them about. Like all good parents, each of them cared deeply for their own children and would go to great lengths to grant their requests, especially when those requests were for a noble cause.

By now, Mr. Tinker and Aadon Blu had secured the raft, which was made easier by the fact that the owner of the raft had a son who was friends with Heavenlee.

All four of them gathered around the raft as citizens of North Munchkin Pier and their children came forward, offering some of this, some of that, and even some of the other.

The most appreciated items were food and refreshment, which came to them in great abundance.

Soon however, they were faced with the dilemma of how to get the raft to the other side of Oz... quickly.

"I wish we had that wagon on a bubble the Royal Magician of Oz let us ride in... remember?" Heavenlee asked her mother.

"Yes," she agreed, "but that was a magic wagon and he used magic on it. We can't, now can we?"

Heavenlee nodded her head sheepishly.

"Yea, but it went really fast," she recalled.

Mr. Tinker took it all in and thought about a river journey. He was certain they could reach the other side of Oz in Winkie Country, but it would take days... and they didn't have days.

The little tinker from Ev thought long and hard about the issue at hand.

"How do we take a raft cross-country?" he thought to himself.

Aadon Blu saw the look in Mr. Tinker's eye and recognized it for what it was… puzzlement.

Fortunately for Mr. Tinker, Aadon had also seen the magic wagon whenever the Royal Magician of Oz visited him in his home in the Pinwheel Fields.

"He called it a Hoverwagon," Aadon explained. "Because it hovers on a bubble of air, only in his case, it was a magic bubble because it never pops."

Aadon watched as a local child came sliding by, riding on a Dragon scale. The shape of the Dragon scale made it look remarkably like one of the petals on the various pinwheels in the Pinwheel Fields

"It's powered by one of my Pinwheels, which itself is enchanted to spin however fast or slow the one riding in it wishes," Aadon continued his explanation.

Slowly, a thought of an idea came to Aadon, much like a fog bank in early autumn, rolling across the riverbanks of the Munchkin River.

Before anyone knew it, Aadon was off exploring the various shops and speaking with whomever would speak to him.

In no time, the blacksmith had agreed to work with the Dragon scales Aadon would provide. He also had some spare rope that he offered to the Caretaker of the Pinwheel Fields.

A local merchant offered some small canvas chairs "for the journey," he suggested.

Another offered provisions and such "for the journey."

Yet another offered to repair a small hole in the deck of the raft.

"Heavenlee, can you ask your friends to gather all the Dragon scales they can find and bring them to me?" Aadon asked his new friend.

Heavenlee was more than happy to help in any way she could, and soon every child in sight was running about, looking for Dragon scales.

Mr. Tinker finally cornered Aadon Blu and questioned him about his idea.

In no time, the little tinker from Ev had his own idea and he too set about talking to the locals about woodworking shops, tools and more rope.

Fortunately for Mr. Tinker and Aadon Blu, rope and tools and woodworking shops were in great abundance in a dockside village.

By the end of twilight, when all the village lamps were lit and North Munchkin Pier glowed warmly, Mr. Tinker and Aadon Blu were hard at work, each at his own task towards making the raft go faster.

Aadon made use of the blacksmith, asking him to punch holes in certain locations along the edges of the Dragon scales.

As it turns out, piercing Dragon scales is a lot harder than it looks and the blacksmith sweated greatly as he struggled to find the proper tool for the job.

Flat chisels and points, all made from the finest iron, took all the pounding he could muster with his heavy smith's hammer and yielded little in return.

Finally, the blacksmith had developed a method with his finest, sharpest punch for cutting neat little holes in the Dragon scales. Fortunately, each hole was as wide as the rope Aadon had been given, making the job so much easier.

Mr. Tinker had the help of several woodworkers as they worked throughout the late evening to produce several cogged wheels of varying size, an equal number of wooden gears, as well as pedals, along with a long pole and crossbeam.

By midnight, Aadon had the Dragon scales lashed together by rope in such a manner as to look nearly identical to one of his pinwheels. Once the long pole and crossbeam were attached to the center of the Dragon scale pinwheel, it was hoisted up into position at the back of the raft by several volunteers.

He then attached four Dragon scales to the raft, one at each corner of the raft, by means of some leftover rope.

In no time at all, Mr. Tinker had assembled the cogged wheels, wooden gears and pedals into an assemblage that looked very much like a bicycle, although no one in the Land of Oz knew what a bicycle was.

When fully assembled, the 'Pinwheel Raft', as Aadon Blu had christened it, was a sight to behold.

Standing nearly eight feet tall, the Dragon scale pinwheel towered over everyone anywhere near it.

It stood proudly, connected by ropes to an odd-looking contraption no one in North Munchkin Pier had ever seen before.

Overall, the Pinwheel Raft was roughly twenty feet long and about ten feet wide, with four small canvas chairs securely roped to the deck in front of the odd-looking contraption.

"Why are there four chairs?" Aadon asked Mr. Tinker.

"I told Harold the Merchant to do that," Darlene informed the two builders of the Pinwheel Raft. "You don't think you're leaving us behind, do you?"

Aadon started to answer, then thought better of the idea. He knew that 'no' was not an option.

By now, it was well past two in the morning and everyone found a villager who would offer food and a warm place to sleep.

Chapter 45
Bon Voyage

The following morning, all four new friends were up and about, going through their morning routines as they thought about the day's journey ahead.

Heavenlee had no trouble falling asleep the night before, but with the first light of the morning sun shining into the room where she slept next to her mother, she was wide awake and ready for the adventure ahead.

Aadon Blu was the same way in the place where he had been offered refuge for the night. With morning's first light, he bounded out of bed and was greeted with a hearty breakfast.

For Mr. Tinker, it was too short a night and he still felt not completely awake as he lumbered about in search of his shoes.

Darlene too found it hard to drag herself out of bed, but found the courage when Heavenlee wouldn't stop bugging her.

Soon, all four friends found themselves gathered together before the Pinwheel Raft, receiving well wishes from all the locals and their children.

A large basket of food was handed up to Aadon Blu as he leaned out to grab it.

He reached out to assist Darlene up the side of the Pinwheel Raft, then assisted Heavenlee, who thanked him warmly.

The three of them sat down as Mr. Tinker sat upon a small cushioned seat astride the odd-looking contraption.

He took the handlebars in hand, twisting one way, then another, noting how the pinwheel turned in the direction that he turned the handlebars.

There was a rousing cheer as all four waved at the adoring crowd.

Mr. Tinker began pedaling the odd-looking contraption and immediately, the large Dragon scale pinwheel began spinning, slowly at first, then faster and faster as Mr. Tinker sped up his pedaling.

With a creaking moan of wood and rope, the Pinwheel Raft lurched forward and the citizens of North Munchkin Pier watched as it slowly headed out of town westward towards the far edges of Oz, in Winkie Country.

Chapter 46
The Kingdom of the Snot Otters

M r. Tinker huffed and puffed as he struggled to
pedal the Pinwheel Raft across the prairie grass
and rolling landscape of Gillikin Country.

The Dragonflies and Damselflies had met up with
them soon after they had gotten underway, but it was clear
that the Pinwheel Raft was not going to be able to keep up
with them.

"Can't you go any faster?" Heavenlee asked,
relaying the question from Odon, who was getting
impatient with the slow progress of the Pinwheel Raft.

In between huffs and puffs, Mr. Tinker explained
that he was going as fast as he could pedal.

Aadon Blu offered to take a turn at pedaling the
contraption and soon was huffing and puffing himself as
the Pinwheel Raft lumbered across the field of purple
grass.

They soon reached a small road of cobblestone that
lead westward and the Pinwheel Raft seemed to gain a
little speed as it glided over the smooth stones. It wasn't
enough speed for Odon and his Herd of Dragonflies, nor
was Anis and her Herd of Damselflies pleased with the
slow progress across Gillikin Country.

"There has to be a way to make this thing go
faster," Darlene suggested. Everyone onboard agreed, but
no one seemed to have an answer.

"If we just had some grease, we could lubricate the Dragon scales and this thing would fly like greased lightning!" Mr. Tinker declared.

Darlene reached into the basket and retrieved a stick of butter.

"Would this do?" she asked.

Mr. Tinker shook his head.

"Only if we had a couple of gallons of it," he replied.

Aadon continued pedaling the geared contraption that powered the Dragon scale pinwheel. The progress was slow and he was soon exhausted by the effort. The Pinwheel Raft then came to a lurching halt as Aadon was unable to pedal anymore.

Sweat was pouring down off of him and Darlene mopped it off with a small towel she had brought along.

The Pinwheel Raft and its occupants had come to rest at a set of crossroads where a small signpost read:

Kingdom of the Snot Otters

The signpost pointed southward and the four of them stared at it for several moments.

"What are Snot Otters?" Heavenlee asked.

"They're friends of mine," Aadon Blu replied. He had met them several years before during his early explorations of the Gillikin countryside.

Aadon pondered the situation while the Dragonflies and Damselflies buzzed about, clearly agitated by the lack of progress they were making.

"If we're gonna get to Drago by day's end, we have got to go faster!" Odon exclaimed.

Heavenlee chose not to translate, but the rest of the occupants of the Pinwheel Raft had a pretty good idea what the Leader of the Dragonflies was upset about.

Just then, an idea floated across Aadon Blu's mind. He had been thinking about the butter and how slippery it was, when inspiration struck.

"Tell your Dragonfly that we need to visit the Snot Otters," Aadon said to Heavenlee, who relayed the message to Odon.

The puzzled looks on the other three friends' faces gave Aadon a bit of a chuckle.

"I have an idea," he said with a mischievous grin.

Heavenlee relayed the message, though Odon was not pleased with the delay.

Darlene offered to pedal the raft and soon they were headed southward towards the Kingdom of the Snot Otters, followed by the Herds of Dragonflies and Damselflies.

Fortunately for Darlene, the Snot Otter's Kingdom was fairly close to the crossroads; and soon she had ceased pedaling as the road came to an abrupt halt in front of a small, fast flowing stream full of large, flat, smooth rocks.

Aadon hopped down and stood before the flowing waters, waiting for something.

"This is the Kingdom of the Snot Otters?" Mr. Tinker asked.

Just then, a large golden salamander, roughly two foot long came lumbering up from beneath a nearby stone in the water.

Aadon looked back at the Pinwheel Raft and smiled.

"Yep, this is it," he declared.

"Aadon Blu, how wonderful to see you once more!" the salamander exclaimed. He was followed by more than a dozen other salamanders of various colors, crawling out from beneath the numerous flat stones within the stream and gathering about the Pinwheel Raft.

"A pleasure to see you too, Your Majesty," Aadon pronounced in as official a tone as he could muster.

"It's a salamander," Mr. Tinker whispered to Darlene and Heavenlee.

Aadon Blu, having heard Mr. Tinker's observation, turned to his friends.

"They prefer to be known as Snot Otters," he informed the occupants of the Pinwheel Raft. "And this is their leader, King Phineas Phlegm."

Aadon Blu introduced everyone to the King of the Snot Otters and soon, every Snot Otter in the kingdom had come out from beneath their homes of stone to greet the visitors.

There was much rejoicing among the Snot Otters as they all knew Aadon Blu and considered him a friend of the kingdom.

Just then, Odon and Anis came flying alongside the Pinwheel Raft and were immediately recognized by King Phineas Phlegm.

"Odon! Anis! What brings you here to our fair kingdom?" he asked happily.

Odon and Anis greeted the King as the other Dragonflies and Damselflies buzzed about the stream, playing with the other Snot Otters.

Odon and Anis explained the dilemma that had brought them to the stream where the Snot Otters lived. They spoke about Drago and the Nome that was enchanting him and how all the other Nomes had fled Oz over the years.

King Phineas Phlegm understood very well the dangers of allowing the last Nome to leave Oz and offered his help without reservations.

"They have crossed the river and are now approaching the mountains of Oogaboo," an advance scout reported, having just returned from his mission.

Odon rejoined the Herd of Dragonflies while Anis conferred with Heavenlee.

"Time's a wasting," she said to the young girl, who agreed with the Leader of the Damselflies.

"So, how can we be of service to your cause, Aadon?" the King asked His friend.

"Well, you are the slipperiest things I have ever come across, what with all that oozing slime you're covered with," Aadon explained. "And somehow, we need to make our raft as slippery as you are."

King Phineas Phlegm thought hard about the issue at hand and was uncertain how his people could help. He waddled about the Pinwheel Raft, looking over the Dragon scales that it rode upon.

Many of his subjects did the same while the Dragonflies and Damselflies buzzed about and the four friends talked among themselves.

"We could coat the Dragon scales with slime, but that wouldn't last very long," the King observed.

Mr. Tinker agreed, remembering his thoughts about the butter.

The King noticed that the Dragon scales were shaped like the shallow bowls He had seen people use whenever they ate.

"Are these Dragon scales?" He asked Aadon Blu, who confirmed that they were. "We could slip inside the scales you have attached to the bottom of that contraption of yours, but how would we get our slime to coat the bottom of the scales?" he pondered out loud.

Darlene, hearing what the King had had said began thinking about her own bowls and platters at home in the Emerald City and was suddenly struck by her own inspiration.

"What we need is a colander," she suggested.

"What's a colander?" the king asked.

"It's a bowl with holes in the bottom," she replied. "I use one in our kitchen to drain washed and cooked food."

Heavenlee recalled in her mind's eye how her mother would drain cooked potatoes before mashing them, or drain the long thin noodles, which she made by hand, after cooking them.

Everyone agreed that Darlene's idea was a good one, but no one knew how to make one. No one that is, except Mr. Tinker, who also knew what a colander was and had his own flash of inspiration.

"If the Dragon scales had holes in the bottom of them, your slime would ooze out the bottom and constantly coat the Dragon scale, making the Pinwheel Raft very slippery," Mr. Tinker explained to the King.

The King had no idea what the new visitor and friend of Aadon Blu was talking about, but He knew Aadon Blu trusted Him, and that was good enough for the King of the Snot Otters.

"Didn't that blacksmith in North Munchkin Pier give you a hammer and sharp punch to use in case we needed to make repairs?" Mr. Tinker asked Aadon Blu.

Aadon nodded his head and understood what Mr. Tinker had in mind. He rummaged about in the large sack that he had been given by the villagers and found the hammer and punch.

The others chatted with King Phineas Phlegm and his subjects while Aadon Blu and Mr. Tinker set about punching holes in the Dragon scales.

Mr. Tinker removed the first Dragon scale and Aadon punched about a dozen holes in the middle of it, then they reattached it to the bottom of the raft.

Mr. Tinker and Aadon Blu repeated their work for the other three Dragon scales until all four Dragon scales now resembled colanders.

King Phineas Phlegm called for His slimiest subjects, whom He called Manny, Moe, Mertrude and Mabel.

"Manny, Moe, Mertrude and Mabel, front and center!" He commanded.

Moments later, two Snot Otters appeared before the King, pledging their service on His behalf.

"You are to ooze slime like never before," was King Phineas Phlegm's simple decree.

Two more appeared moments later, pledging their service as well.

His four willing subjects heartedly agreed and were soon laying snugly, each in one of the four punctured Dragon scales upon which the Pinwheel Raft rode upon.

"Farwell my friends!" Aadon Blu exclaimed as he boarded the Pinwheel Raft, leaving behind the Kingdom of the Snot Otters.

Mr. Tinker took the controls of the pedaling contraption and slowly maneuvered the Pinwheel Raft back northwards towards the crossroads and the signpost.

Chapter 47
The Ace of Hearts

Heavenlee shouted gleefully as the Pinwheel Raft glided smoothly and very rapidly across the purple grasslands of Gillikin Country. She was thoroughly exhilarated by the whole experience and smiled up at her mother, who was sitting next to her in one of the four canvas chairs.

"It's just like when we rode in the Hoverwagon to watch Jamie battle that hot dog!" she shouted above the rushing wind.

Darlene laughed, as did her daughter, and the two of them held on tight as the Pinwheel Raft continued its smooth glide across the countryside.

In fact, the ride was so smooth and so fast that the passing landscape was becoming a blur.

Mr. Tinker was pedaling at a leisurely rate while the pinwheel spun at a constant rate, pushing the Pinwheel Raft across hillocks, small streams, and cobblestone roads. He marveled at how well the slime from the Snot Otters riding below within the Dragon scales had lubricated the bottom of the raft, making it glide almost effortlessly towards Winkie Country, where Drago and his captor were now approaching the mountains of Oogaboo.

As for the Snot Otters, they found it relatively easy to fulfill their King's command. Each had begun oozing slime so fast that wherever the Pinwheel Raft had traveled, a slimy trail of ooze and slime followed behind, leaving its mark on the purple landscape of Gillikin Country.

Both Odon and his Herd of Dragonflies, along with Anis and her Herd of Damselflies, were now very pleased by the progress of their compatriots, who seemed to have figured out a way to go really fast.

In fact, some of the older Dragonflies and Damselflies found it difficult to keep up so that the Herds became strung out into a long line of insects flying low across the hills and hollows of Oz.

In no time, they had passed the Pinwheel Fields and were fast approaching the middle of Gillikin Country.

By noontime, they were passing between the Dark Forest of Gillikin Country and the Northern Mountain Range of Gillikin Country when Mr. Tinker called for a break. He had also wanted to take some measurements with his Lunar Astrolabe in hopes of fixing their position and calculating how much further they had to go.

Everyone was glad to take a break, including the Dragonflies and Damselflies, all of whom were quite in need of some rest.

Heavenlee looked northward and saw the great mountains that made up the Great Northern Mountains of Gillikin Country.

"Aren't those the Great Northern Mountains, Mom?" Heavenlee asked her mother.

"I think so," was her mother's response.

"Yes, those are the Great Northern Mountains, where the Royal Magician of Oz and his family live," Aadon Blu informed them.

With that information in hand, Heavenlee rummaged about in a small backpack that she carried with her throughout the adventure her and her mother had set out upon many weeks before.

"Here it is!" she declared as the young girl pulled out a small paper box containing a deck of playing cards. She looked through the cards until she found just the right one. It just so happened to be the Ace of Hearts, Heavenlee's favorite card.

Holding the card between her two fingers and thumb, Heavenlee took aim at the Great Northern Mountains.

"What are you doing?" Darlene asked her daughter.

Heavenlee stopped to explain herself.

"Remember when Jamie showed me how to throw playing cards, like he did when he defeated the Shadow Demon?" she asked her mother.

Darlene remembered back to the battle on top of Mount Munch and how young Jamie Diggs had thrown a playing card into the murky blackness of shadow and smoke that was the Shadow Demon as part of his plan to defeat it. She remembered how Heavenlee had asked him weeks later how he had thrown that card and he had taught her how.

She nodded her head in agreement.

"Well, he gave me these cards and told me that if I was ever near his home, to toss him a card and he would drop by for a visit," she continued her explanation.

With that, the young girl heaved the card forward with all her might, sending it spinning across the landscape, heading northward towards the mountains and growing smaller by the moment, until they could no longer see it. She smiled broadly and jumped down from the deck of the Pinwheel Raft.

Chapter 48
The Magic Door

Jamie Diggs had been tinkering around most of the day, working on some effects he was preparing for a performance he hoped to arrange for Princess Dorothy. They were mostly sleight-of-hand and misdirection effects that he knew would amuse the little farm girl from Kansas.

"It's so wonderful how you can perform magic without using magic," she had commented once when he was showing her a simple coin routine.

Now, he had put together a number of effects that he felt flowed together fairly well. His great grandfather, the former Wizard of Oz, had praised him for his choice and the order he had chosen.

"Don't forget the patter," he reminded his young protégé.

Jamie thought about the words he would use during his routine. As he practiced, something caught his eye and drew his attention.

Through a nearby large window came a playing card, spinning rapidly until it nearly reached the young magician, then it fluttered slowly down until he reached out and plucked it from mid-air.

It was the Ace of Hearts and Jamie Diggs recognized it as his friend's favorite card.

"Looks like you've got mail," O.Z. Diggs told his great grandson.

Jamie smiled and nodded in agreement. He thought about his friend Heavenlee, who had done so much for his mother and his best friend Buddy when they first met in Oz more than five years ago.

"Mom! Dad! I'll be back later!" Jamie yelled across the room as he darted out the door and into the front yard.

After five years as the official Royal Magician of Oz, James and Amanda had grown quite accustomed to their son's occasional rapid departures as he set off on one adventure or another.

For now, Jamie Diggs was in search of one thing and he soon found it.

There at his feet was a unique feat of magic he had created several years ago in order to travel around Oz in a timely manner.

He had called it his Magic Door and it was a large oak-wood door, complete with a large glass doorknob and an even larger brass door knocker in the middle of it. It was laying flat on the ground and the Royal Magician of Oz approached it.

"Heavenlee please," the Royal Magician of Oz spoke in a tone of great confidence as he addressed the Magic Door.

He reached down and grasped the large brass door knocker, then rapped the wood three times.

"Who is it?" came a voice from the other side of the door.

"It's Jamie! Can I come in?" came Jamie's reply.

The young magician watched as the large oak-wood door was opened from the other side. The door swung down into the ground, revealing a bright yellow light. He proceeded to walk down into the open doorway and found himself standing in a yellow field at the foot of the massive mountains which border the province of Oogaboo. He was not alone.

217

Chapter 49
Follow The Yellow Slick Road

When Aadon Blu took over the pedaling duties after their mid-day break, he decided to push the Pinwheel Raft to its limits. He was curious how well the Dragon scale pinwheel could really operate; and he was also aware of how close Drago and Kaliko were to reaching Oogaboo, where he had heard of Nomes leaving Oz through a way out in the small province of Oz.

If the other occupants of the Pinwheel Raft thought Mr. Tinker had pedaled them fast, they hadn't seen anything yet.

Aadon Blu wound up the Dragon scale pinwheel as fast as he could on the pedaling contraption. It was exhilarating to see how fast he could get the raft going.

"The Snot Otter's slime is working really good, ain't it?" Aadon shouted down at the seated occupants, all of whom were hanging on for dear lives.

Even Mr. Tinker, who had travelled back from the Moon at a phenomenal speed, was greatly impressed at how well everything worked together.

He found himself studying the motion of the gearings, working out the math of it all and looking at improvements for the next model. His craftsmanship and skills had really shined through in the tiny details that ensured it ran smoothly.

The little tinker from Ev leaned down to look at the Dragon scale runners, each with a sliming, oozing Snot Otter inside, fulfilling their King's command.

He looked back up at Aadon Blu, who looked to be no more winded than when he started his shift at the helm of the Pinwheel Raft, and gave him a thumbs-up.

Within an hour, they had crossed over into the predominantly yellow countryside of Winkie Country and by mid-day, had crossed the Winkie River with barely a ripple in the flowing waters.

The Herds of Dragonflies and Damselflies had been left behind almost immediately after the raft's departure from their resting place in sight of the Great Northern Mountains. They came to a halt and gathered together to confer and decide on their next course of action.

"Now what do we do?" Odon asked his sister.

"Just keep following that trail of slime from the Snot Otters," Anis replied." She flew off ahead of the Herds about a hundred yards or so and found the trail of slime from the Pinwheel Raft.

"See?" she announced to the gathering of Dragonflies and Damselflies that had formed a large circle around Odon and Anis.

An odd thought flashed across her mind.

"It's kind of yellowish in color and very slick," Anis said as she hovered over the yellowish slime laying on the ground and forming a wide trail that led due west.

"As long as we follow the yellow slick road, we'll get to our destination, which is Drago and the last Nome in Oz" Anis announced.

"Let me get this straight. You want us to follow the yellow slick road?" he asked.

Anis buzzed her wings in agreement.

"Yes, just follow the yellow slick road," she said in an almost musical tone of voice.

"Follow the yellow slick road," another Damselfly nearby sang, followed by a Dragonfly singing the phrase.

"Follow the yellow slick road…" two more Damselflies sang out.

"STOP!" Odon shouted as loudly as he could. The effect was an almost eerie silence, punctuated only by the low humming sound of over a thousand Dragonflies and an equal number of Damselflies.

"We get it!" he shouted to the now silent throngs of hovering insects.

Odon was not particularly fond of singing, nor of songs in general. He thought them to be frivolous and a waste of time.

The Damselflies let out a combined roar of laughter that soon took over the Dragonflies as all rejoiced in their mission and the fun they were having while doing it.

Chapter 50
No Stopping A Dragon

Kaliko sat atop Drago, as he had done since his capture of the beast, and surveyed the approaching mountains that surrounded and shielded the Land of Oogaboo from the rest of Oz.

He had commanded Drago to do his bidding, which included refilling his water flask, picking food from nearby Lunchpail Trees, which always seemed to contain exactly what he wanted to eat; and continually moving westward towards the Land of Oogaboo.

At his side, the Lunar Gems had enabled the former Chief Steward to the Nome King to increase and maintain his control of the Dragon. Unfortunately for Kaliko, they also seemed to affect him in a more personal way, clouding his judgment and vision of purpose.

Since passing the Pinwheel Fields yesterday, Kaliko's thoughts had drifted away from finding and returning the Nomes to their own dominion, which bordered the Land of Ev and the Deadly Desert.

For reasons known only to the Lunar Gems, they had taken the Nome's overwhelming loneliness and corrupted it into a lust for power and wealth.

Now, he thought only of conquest and restoring the Dominion of the Nomes to its former glory and wealth… with him returning as the Nome King.

Such were the thoughts on Kaliko's mind as Drago lumbered slowly towards the borders of Oogaboo.

As for Drago, his thoughts lingered solely on his mate, Dragonelli and his children, the Dragonettes. His will to resist however, had been struck down as soon as Kaliko had addressed him with his Voice of Command. No other Nome had been able to achieve this feat and Drago was unable to resist any command given to him by the Nome riding him.

He had been grateful for the night's rest, if only to prolong his possible departure from the Land of Oz... and his family.

Kaliko began searching the mountain's profile, looking for the little inlet that led towards Ozsnobolis and on to the Land of Oogaboo.

He was certain they were nearly upon it when he realized that an odd looking contraption was approaching from the east... and doing so with remarkable speed.

Within five minutes or so, the Pinwheel Raft had come to a complete halt, directly in the path of the lumbering Dragon.

Mr. Tinker stood up from his canvas seat and looked directly into the eyes of Kaliko, sitting atop Drago and no more than twenty feet away. He watched as the Nome said something to the Dragon, then realized that the Dragon had no intention, or even a will to stop... or even slow down.

"Abandon ship!" he cried out.

Darlene grabbed her daughter and leapt from the Pinwheel Raft, followed by Aadon Blu, Mr. Tinker and all four Snot Otters.

Drago's blank eyes didn't even see the Pinwheel Raft as he plodded roughshod over it, leaving behind a pile of lumber, rope and Dragon scales, as well as four very frightened people.

Chapter 51
Who Is It?

No sooner had Drago made the Pinwheel Raft into rubble when Heavenlee heard a knock at the door. She turned around to find a large oak-wood door, bearing a glass doorknob, laying among the yellow clover that covered the field which sprawled out from the Mountains of Oogaboo.

Unable to think of any other response, Heavenlee spoke to the door.

"Who is it?" she asked.

"It's Jamie! Can I come in?" came her friend's reply.

Heavenlee reached down and grasped the glass doorknob. Turning it slowly, she lifted up and opened the door until it lay upon the yellow clover, revealing blue skies and a young boy walking up into Winkie Country.

Heavenlee and Jamie Diggs embraced warmly as friends often do and soon, her mother joined in the greetings for a friend.

Aadon waited a moment or two, knowing the bond his friend and Heavenlee shared from the stories the Royal Magician of Oz told him over the last few years.

Soon, Jamie Diggs was embracing the Caretaker of the Pinwheel Fields and jabbing him in the ribs.

"What's this? Have you abandoned your post?" the Royal Magician of Oz asked the Caretaker of the Pinwheel Fields.

Aadon tried to explain his need for an adventure, "and besides, they weren't spinning, so I figured you weren't home."

Jamie's reaction was one of happiness in knowing that his friend was happy and content with his Life. He looked over at the oddly-dressed stranger and lifted an eyebrow.

Aadon took the hint and made the introductions.

"Jamie, may I present Mr. Tinker, of the Land of Ev, who's been away a while," he said in a most official tone.

Jamie smiled at Mr. Tinker and the two shook hands warmly.

"Are you the same Mr. Tinker who built Tik-Tok; the Mechanical Army of Oz?" he inquired.

With that, the little tinker from Ev went into a rather long soliloquy about his adventures on the Moon and his most recent ones back in Oz.

Jamie tried to listen, but was soon distracted by an odd sight lumbering away from them.

It was a Dragon, being ridden by a Nome and headed away from a substantial pile of rubble.

"Having problems with your Dragon?" Jamie said, finally managing to get a word in.

"Oh goodness gracious!" Darlene exclaimed. "In all the excitement, we forgot that we were nearly run over by a Dragon!"

The next half hour was spent bringing the Royal Magician of Oz up to date on what had happened and what they were trying to do.

"So, where are the Dragonflies and Damselflies?" Jamie asked the assembled group of friends.

"In all the excitement, it seems we also forgot about them as well," Darlene confessed. Everyone agreed, even the Snot Otters, who had returned from visiting a nearby stream to moisten up and refresh their slime. They were fairly certain they weren't going to be doing any more sliming anytime soon.

Chapter 52
The Dragonflies and Damselflies Arrival

"So this pile of rubble was once a Pinwheel Raft?" Jamie asked his friend Aadon.

"And a pretty nice one too!" Darlene spoke up before Aadon could answer. Everyone agreed.

As they described the role of the Snot Otters, Jamie Diggs looked over the pile of lumber, rope and Dragon scales.

"This I have got to see!" he shouted.

The Royal Magician of Oz gathered his thoughts together and tried to envision what a pinwheel raft would look like. He wasn't certain if it would assemble that way or another, but it didn't matter as he spoke his words of magic.

"Wham, bam, alikazam!" he nearly whispered. "Pinwheel Raft…"

For moment, there was nothing but silence. Then, the rubble began to vibrate and spread apart, rearranging itself until it was once more the Pinwheel Raft.

Mr. Tinker was dumbfounded by the display of magic. He had seen so little of it when he lived in Oz long ago, and now, it was happening right in front of him.

The rest were quite accustomed to it by now, having been around the Royal Magician of Oz for the last few years.

"Wow!" Jamie Diggs exclaimed.

He looked over the large raft, glancing beneath the deck at the Dragon scale runners. He spied the Snot Otters taking their place back inside the Dragon scale runners. The odd-looking contraption that powered the Dragon scale pinwheel caught Jamie's attention.

"Where did you get a bicycle from?" Jamie asked Mr. Tinker before he realized that the whole contraption was made of wood and rope.

"Ingenious…" the young magician complimented Mr. Tinker as he looked up at the Dragon scale pinwheel that Aadon Blu had contracted.

"First, it was abandoning your post. Now, you're stealing my pinwheel secrets?!" Jamie said in a false mocking voice. He jabbed Aadon in the ribs once more, laughing as he did so.

The two exchanged a few more laughs before the situation caught up with them.

Where's Drago and the Nome?" Heavenlee asked.

It suddenly dawned on the entire group that, in all the excitement, they had forgotten about the most important thing of all… Drago.

Heavenlee gestured towards the trail of yellowish slime, which was pointing towards the highest peaks of the Oogaboo Mountains.

Just then, a low humming sound came wafting in over the breeze, due east and approaching fast.

Jamie Diggs watched as the Herds of Dragonflies and Damselflies came flying by, encircling the gathering and coming to rest among the high grasses of the Winkie prairie.

Chapter 53
Libertatum!

Odon and Anis spoke to the Royal Magician of Oz through Heavenlee, who was all too happy to help out.

They explained their plan to him, retelling the history of the Nomes that had left before and how Kaliko was the last Nome in Oz.

"The tall one there, in the odd, old-looking clothes claims he brought some rocks back from the Moon. He called them The Lunar Gems," Odon explained as he pointed his thorax at Mr. Tinker. "They have magic within them and we are certain we can claim some of that magic to bring the Nomes back to Oz."

Jamie thought about what the Dragonflies and Damselflies were proposing to do and a disturbing thought crossed his mind. He furrowed his brow and looked at Odon, who was hovering at eye-level with the young boy.

"You realize that what you want to do may be considered doing magic?" the Royal Magician of Oz asked the Leader of the Dragonflies.

"I do, but to do nothing would risk harm to our lands and those who live on them," he replied.

"Or in them," Anis added. "Remember, Nomes are our cousins too."

Jamie thought hard about the dilemma the Dragonflies and Damselflies were in. He was certain Princess Ozma would understand, but he didn't want to speak on Her behalf. That would have been beyond his authority... and Jamie Diggs respected authority.

Once more, inspiration struck the young magician and he puzzled a way out of the Dilemma of the Dragonflies and Damselflies.

"Gather your Herds together," he said through Heavenlee, "and I will perform a bit of magic upon you to enhance the power of the Lunar Gems as you take some of it for yourselves. This way, you will operate under my authority as the Royal Magician of Oz and Her Majesty's Royal Decree will be obeyed, since I am allowed to perform magic."

With that, the word went out to the Damselflies and Dragonflies to gather together near the Pinwheel Raft "for a bit of magic," Anis and Odon informed their Herds.

In no time, the Herds were all together in a single circle which spanned well over a hundred feet.

Darlene and her daughter sat back on the Pinwheel Raft, with Aadon Blu and Mr. Tinker beside them as the Royal Magician of Oz added his own bit of magic to the magic that was about to be unleashed on the Gnome of Oz.

"Wham, bam, alikazam! Lunar Gems Libertatum!" he exclaimed so that all the Dragonflies and Damselflies gathered together could hear.

With those words, a green mist enveloped the Herds and imbued them with magic and purpose.

Soon, the Herds were off to follow the yellow slick road and embrace their destiny.

"What did 'libertatum' mean?" Heavenlee asked her mother.

Darlene shrugged her shoulders, but Mr. Tinker, who had been well versed in Latin from long ago knew what it meant.

"It's Latin for 'Liberty'," he said definitively.

The gathered friends boarded the Pinwheel Raft and followed the trail of crushed field grasses and brush left in Drago's wake.

Jamie Diggs was most impressed by the operation of the Pinwheel Raft, though he clearly preferred his Hoverwagon.

"Less work," he muttered to himself as he watched Mr. Tinker pedaling the odd-looking contraption he had mistaken for a bicycle.

In a matter of minutes though, they had caught up with the wayward Dragon and his captor, who was now thoroughly surrounded by the Herds of Dragonflies and Damselflies.

Odon had gathered together with his sister, Anis and refined their plan, now that their target was in sight.

"Corkscrew up, then brush along the pouch and leave a dozen behind for the Dragon," Anis suggested. Odon agreed completely and the two of them set out to inform their troops of the plan of battle.

Drago lurched forward, step by step, as he had been commanded to do for the last two days. His head hung low and visions of Dragonelli and his Dragonettes flashed through his memory as the Nome urged him on.

Just then, a low buzzing sound appeared near his ear and soon dozens, then hundreds, and finally thousands of Dragonflies and Damselflies began spiraling around the massive Dragon in a tight corkscrew spiral that brought the flying insects up around the feet and legs of Kaliko, who was suddenly powerless to do anything but swat at the annoying creatures.

The Lunar Gems, which had held sway over the massive Dragon, were powerless to affect the small flying insects that now circled around the former Nome King.

One by one, each Damselfly and Dragonfly flew past the small white pouch attached to a belt worn by the Nome.

Each time a Dragonfly or Damselfly brushed his or her wings up against the soft cotton fabric, their wings would light up like a firefly. The only difference was that their wings would remain glowing, rather than blinking on and off, like a Firefly.

"Is that the magic from the Lunar Gems making their wings glow like that?" Heavenlee asked her friend, Jamie Diggs as she pointed towards the ever-growing Herds of glowing Dragonflies and Damselflies.

Jamie nodded in agreement. He watched as the herds peeled off and headed south by southwest towards Quadling Country where the Nome tunnel behind the Magic Waterfall led to a waterfall entrance into the Great Outside.

"Where are they going?" Darlene asked the Royal Magician of Oz.

"They are going to liberate the Gnome of Oz," he replied, then furrowed his brow once more. "Or are they the Nomes of Oz?"

Chapter 54
The Plan Of The Dragonflies

Anis and Odon, followed by just over a thousand Dragonflies and Damselflies, made their way across Oz in record time. The Emerald City flashed by in a blur as they crossed the breadth of verdant green in the blink of an eye.

Within an hour, they had made it to the southern Quadling Country and the Great Waterfall, where a Nome tunnel behind the falling waters led to a waterfall entrance in the Great Outside. There, all the Nomes had gone and been transformed into Gnome.

"That magician's magic is beyond anything we've ever seen!" Odon declared as the Herd of Dragonflies gathered beside the falling waters and waited for the Heard of Damselflies too arrive.

Their wait was only a minute or so as Anis and her Heard of Damselflies arrived in mass.

"I have never flown that fast… ever!" Anis exclaimed. Odon could tell that his sister was quite exhilarated by the crossing of Oz.

To be honest, he was equally as thrilled and suspected that every Dragonfly and Damselfly felt the same.

The Royal Magician of Oz's magic was indeed quite powerful, especially given the cause for which it was created; that of liberty.

Brother and sister led the way between curtains of water and countless falling drops until the water had been cleared and the tunnel stood just ahead.

Every Dragonfly and Damselfly now followed their leaders into the darkness of the Nome tunnel and embarked on what each of them hoped would be the return of the Nomes and the salvation of Oz.

Moments later, every one of them braved the falling waters of the other waterfall and made their way into the Great Outside.

The waterfall happened to be located in a small state park in the middle of New York State and was known as The Falls.

"That was quick!" Anis shouted at her brother, who was too distracted trying to get his bearings.

Behind him, both Herds were now in full force and eager to go.

Odon knew now what he must say to the combined forces of the Damselflies and Dragonflies.

"You each have a Nome that you have visited before. Seek him," Odon proclaimed.

"Or her!" Anis interrupted.

Odon flashed a brief glare at her, then resumed his proclamation.

"Seek them and transfer your magic, by the power of the Lunar Gems!" Odon said proudly. "Then invite them home and lead the way back!"

The pride within his voice and the compassion of their mission combined to give every member of the Herds the overwhelming confidence it would take to rescue the Nomes of Oz.

In a single moment, the entire combined forces of the Herds exploded outwards in all directions, each

Damselfly and Dragonfly aiming for the one gnome they each knew as Nome.

In a flash, they had dispersed to the four corners of the land, seeking out gnome and bringing their magic to bear upon them.

Gnorm the Gnome stood fast and solid as stone at his post, which was no surprise to him. The yard of the old Hoosier farmhouse was quite as the family had taken a trip to town for things of need.

The only sound he could hear was the barking of a lone dog, far off in the distance.

It was past mid-afternoon and Gnorm enjoyed this time of day at this time of year.

The sun was shining down from a clear blue sky and the gnome holding the pipe thought he heard a familiar buzz from a green Dragonfly.

Odon flashed by the familiar gnome he had visited numerous times before.

"He's faded a bit," the green Dragonfly thought to himself.

Gnorm the Gnome stared at the flying insect now hovering inches from his nose. He thought maybe the wings were glowing, but he wasn't sure.

Just then, the green Dragonfly brushed his wings up against the nose of Gnorm and a strange thing happened.

Gnorm felt a tingle that ran throughout his stone body, as though he had been struck by lightning... again.

The green Dragonfly backed away in mid-air and observed the results of his actions.

Gnorm the Gnome inhaled deeply and felt a surge of Life course through his body. He felt his arms and legs twitch ever so slightly and a desire to scratch his nose overwhelmed him.

For the first time since his escape from Oz, he moved... and his first action was to scratch his nose.

Gnorm looked around a remembered. He remembered his Life before the darkness and the light that ushered his entrance into the Great Outside.

Flashes of memory rushed over him like waves on the Nonestic Ocean, which surrounded the entire fairy lands ruled over by Queen Lurline.

"Please, return to Oz with me... and be free again," Odon said proudly. He wasn't quite sure the little garden gnome understood him, but he hoped the Nome within would.

In no time, Gnorm the Gnome left the little yard of the Hoosier farmhouse in a flash of green light that enveloped him when Odon landed upon his pointed cap and spoke a single word.

"Oz," Odon said simply, and in that green flash, Gnorm the Gnome became Norm the Nome and found himself back in Oz at the base of the Mountains of Oogaboo, where Jamie had enchanted the Herds of Dragonflies and Damselflies earlier.

The gnome with the fishing pole, who had discovered his name to be Ruggedo, listened for the sounds that told him children were approaching. For him, their playful laughter and joyous games gave him great joy, as did their desire to share their secrets with him.

Ruggedo rejoiced in his role as Keeper of the Secrets and was busily listening for their approach when another sound invaded his domain. It was the buzzing of two Dragonflies and a Damselfly; and they were flittering about and catching his eye.

"You check out the one over there, Speedo," Anis commanded, "and you check out the other one, Snail."

Snail darted across the road and into the yard of the house across the street where the gnome holding a staff stood steadfast and immovable as always.

The blue Dragonfly approached the fishing gnome and landed gently on the end of the fishing pole. The effect was immediate as Ruggedo was overwhelmed by a wave of intense emotions as memories of his former Life came rushing over him.

He recalled with great fear; visions of his defeat at the hands of the Scarecrow, who tossed eggs at him; which were provided by Billina the Hen.

Another memory of eggs being hurled by Quox the Dragon gave him even greater reason to fear for what was happening to him. He soon felt the quiver of muscles, aching to move and put down the fishing pole he had held for as long as he could recall.

"Please, return to Oz with me… and be free again," Speedo recited, assured that the Nome would agree to return home.

"Be gone!!!" Ruggedo shouted as loudly as he could as he swung his fishing pole at the blue Dragonfly, barely missing him.

Speedo was instantly convinced that this Nome had no desire to return to Oz. He suddenly found himself unsure as to what to do next.

Odon hadn't instructed them about what to do if the Nome wants to stay.

The blue Dragonfly decided to hang around for awhile, just in case the Nome changed his mind.

Across the street, he watched as the Nome holding a staff and his friend Snail, vanish in a flash of green light.

Anis looked about for the garden gnome playing a flute and was puzzled that she wasn't in her usual spot.

A quick check around the yard and Anis soon located the flute-playing garden gnome, near the back porch where several plastic pink flamingos had come to roost.

She landed gently upon the flute; and like all the other gnome, the flute-playing gnome was overcome by the joy of Life and the feelings of movement and freedom.

A song came fluttering out of the flute as the Nome rejoiced in his newly found freedom. It sounded gently over the breeze and echoed across the neighborhood.

"Please, return to Oz with me… and be free again," Anis invited the joyous Nome, who gladly agreed.

Moments later, the flute-playing Nome and Anis returned to the field of yellow prairie grasses by the Mountains of Oogaboo.

Speedo now found himself alone in the company of one seriously angry Nome.

Chapter 55
Mercy Is Mightier Than Revenge

Once the magic of the Lunar Gems had been nearly depleted, Kaliko's control over Drago had evaporated and the former Chief Steward to King Ruggedo found himself tossed aside from his perch atop the Dragon. He suddenly found himself on the wrong side of a seriously angry Dragon.

He threw the pouch containing the Lunar Gems at the Dragon, but to no avail.

It took a passionate plea from Heavenlee to convince Drago not to destroy the now powerless Nome. He was filled with rage over being enchanted and controlled by Kaliko and thought to punish the Nome for his Evil deed.

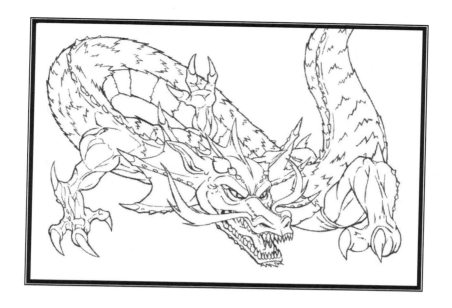

"Heavenlee is right," Aadon assured the Dragon. "Anger only makes us weaker, not stronger… and mercy is mightier than revenge."

Drago saw the wisdom in their words, as well as the fear in Kaliko's eyes, and he decided to forgive and rejoice in his freedom.

Besides, he had a family to return to.

"I must leave you now and return home to my mate and children," Drago informed Heavenlee. "They have no idea where I have gone to and must be worried sick over my absence."

Heavenlee assured her friend Drago that they were doing well and knew of his abduction by the Nome.

"When you get home, be sure to ask Dragonelli about her bargain with the Dragonflies and Damselflies," Heavenlee informed Drago.

After several tearful farewells, Drago expended his mighty wings and flapped hard, lifting himself into the air and gliding eastward towards the Eastern peaks… and his home and family.

After his departure, Nomes and Dragonflies, or Damselflies, began appearing in the field where the Pinwheel Raft had set down for the evening, each set heralded by a bright green flash.

Waiting for them was a gathering of friends, sitting around a campfire, watching the sunset and worrying about the fate of the Nomes and their Liberators, the Dragonflies and Damselflies.

Once each Nome had returned and regained his or her senses, the Royal Magician of Oz welcomed them back to Oz and led each one over to a small mound of stones where Kaliko had taken refuge.

After about a dozen or so Nomes had returned, Norm the Nome appeared in a flash of green light and shout of joy, followed very quickly by a Nome carrying a wooden staff and another holding a flute and all equally glad to be back in Oz.

Mr. Tinker conferred with Jamie Diggs and Aadon Blu while Darlene and Heavenlee set about preparing for a night's rest.

"Kaliko told me he got here through a tunnel he dug all the way from the Dominion of the Nomes, beneath the Deadly Desert," Mr. Tinker recalled being told by Kaliko when they worked on Enarc Brenkert. "Perhaps he can escort his fellow Nomes back to their Dominion?"

Aadon and Jamie agreed that it was a good idea, but each wondered how long it would take for all the Nomes to return.

By the following morning, nearly all of the Nomes had returned to Oz. Only a handful remained behind, though one of them was known by all who were now gathered with Kaliko and wondering what to do now.

"What about Ruggedo?" many of the Nomes asked out loud.

There was great concern among the Nomes that the reason they had left in the first place was because Ruggedo had vanished into the Great Outside long ago. His absence had caused a great deal of turmoil, since being a leaderless mob had left them with no purpose and no reason to hang around Oz.

Chapter 56
Fumbled Eggs

Ruggedo looked about and saw no sign of the annoying little Dragonfly that had somehow enchanted him and freed him from his stony disposition. He noticed the red glow of the setting sun and decided that at nightfall, he would do a little exploring, now that he was mobile.

An hour later, evening twilight had faded and the stars were in full display above Ruggedo's pointed cap.

The little garden Nome put down his fishing pole and walked slowly about the yard, first exploring every crook and nanny of the front yard, followed by the back yard. The rising full Moon made his exploration easier, though when the neighborhood cat showed up, he was uncertain how to deal with it, now that he wasn't solid stone anymore.

By morning, Ruggedo had resumed his station at the cement pond, fishing pole in hand and a nice scratch upon his nose where the cat had decided to swat him.

It was a Saturday morning and several of the local girls had gathered together in the yard to play. They were trying out a new game that involved tossing eggs high into the air at each other and trying to catch them without breaking them.

All had gone well until Zoe went to catch an egg that had been thrown very high up and very far.

Unfortunately for Ruggedo, Zoe fumbled the egg and it came crashing down on top of his pointed hat.

"Ahhh, you missed!" shouted one of the other girls as they headed for the back yard to continue their game.

At first, Ruggedo felt nothing, then a slow trickle of egg yolks came dripping down onto his nose.

For the first time since his arrival in the front yard of the old Hoosier farmhouse, Ruggedo felt pain. It was an intense pain and the former Nome King recalled why he feared eggs in the first place.

"Eggs are poison to Nomes!" he shouted in his mind.

The blue Dragonfly, who had found refuge in a small bush for the night, came buzzing forward, sensing that something was wrong.

Ruggedo's nose was on fire, or so it must have felt like, and he screamed out in pain.

"Oooowww!!!" cried the little garden Nome.

"What was that?" one of the young girls asked as they all came running around to the front yard to see who had yelled.

There was no one in the front yard but a blue Dragonfly and the little garden gnome, who was now covered in slowly dripping egg yolk.

They all shrugged their shoulders and headed to the back yard for more play time.

The blue Dragonfly saw his chance and made his offer once more.

"Please, return to Oz with me... and be free again," Speedo offered.

Ruggedo knew that this was his only chance to escape the pain and the poison that eggs brought to his kind. He nodded, unwilling to speak and risk the young girls returning and discovering his secret.

Speedo landed gently on the fishing pole and in an instant, a green flash enveloped both Nome and

Dragonfly, transporting them back to the field of yellow grass and his fellow Nomes.

Chapter 57
Gnome or Nome

"Why didn't you want to return to Oz? " Kaliko asked his former King.

Ruggedo furrowed his brow and recalled his days as Nome King.

"When I was King, I was consumed with the quest for power and wealth," he explained. "I thought of nothing else. Even when I was defeated and made to drink from the Water of Oblivion, somehow, my memories came back, as well as my lust for power. Even before my days as Ruggedo, when I was Roquat of the Rocks, all I cared for was power and wealth!"

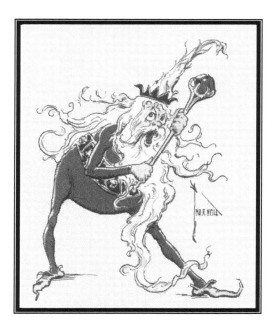

Everyone listened in as Ruggedo explained his dilemma to his former Chief Steward, Kaliko.

"When I finally escaped Oz, I found myself transported to a wonderful place where I was treated like one of the family. Children showered me with Love and made me Keeper of the Secrets," Ruggedo explained. "The only thing I ever missed was being able to talk… and move."

Heavenlee couldn't imagine not being able to move or speak. She squeezed her mother's arm and hugged her tight.

"Now, I'm back here where all my darkest visions reside," the former Nome King confessed.

Kaliko assured him that "this time, things will be different. I promise!"

All the other Nomes shouted in agreement. They too wanted their King back.

Ruggedo let out a soft sigh, then relented and accepted his fate. He would once again become the Nome King… and hopefully stay out of trouble this time.

"My only regret is that I couldn't bring my G back from the Great Outside," the Nome King lamented. Every Nome there but one understood exactly what their King was sad about, and almost all of them agreed.

Even Jamie Diggs understood somewhat, having had a similar conversation with his mother about the letter G.

With that, the large gathering of newly freed Nomes made their way eastward towards the Deadly Desert and the small tunnel Kaliko had carved out over so long a time.

It would take days for them to make it through to the Dominion of the Nomes.

Meanwhile, Jamie Diggs bid his friends farewell and stepped back through his Magic Door and his home high in the Great Northern Mountains of Gillikin Country. He had to report back to his parents, then make an official report to Princess Ozma regarding his actions over the last few days.

Heavenlee and Darlene suggested that Mr. Tinker join them as they made their way home to the Emerald City.

"Besides, didn't you say you wanted to present Princess Ozma with the Lunar Gems?" Heavenlee asked Mr. Tinker.

"Can you drop me off at my place? " Aadon Blu chimed in.

It was agreed that the Pinwheel Raft would escort Heavenlee and her mother home to Emerald City, with a slight detour to drop Aadon Blu off at home.

Mr. Tinker was pleased that he would be able to fulfill his original purpose, at least in part, since King Pastoria was no more, and his daughter, Princess Ozma was now the Royal Ruler of Oz.

He was also pleased at being given the Pinwheel Raft for his own personal use once he had completed his Royal visit. He was certain that he now had a means to cross the Impassable Desert and return to his home in the Land of Ev.

Chapter 58
Home

The reunion of Drago with Dragonelli and the Dragonettes was as joyful as any reunion had ever been in the Land of Oz. Love consumed Castle Nogard in its embrace and made its way down to Lake Nogard, where the Herds of Dragonflies and Damselflies gathered in the cattails and lily pads that was their home, resuming their daily leisure of racing among the reeds and the Singular Oak.

For them, the task had been completed and now, their prolonged discussions focused mainly on more trivial matters, such as the weather and who was faster, Dragonflies or Damselflies.

Drago had asked Dragonelli about the bargain she had made.

"The Dragonflies and Damselflies offered their services of liberating you from that Nome on the agreement that the Dragonettes would no longer eat the cattails and lily pads of Lake Nogard, which they consider their home" she explained carefully, making sure that Drago understood the bargain she had struck with the Dragonflies and Damselflies.

"Seems like a small price to pay for my freedom… besides, there's plenty of other food growing about the countryside," he said.

"That's what I said!" she exclaimed to herself. It was then that she realized Drago knew the importance of the bargain.

For Drago, it was all Love and joy to be among his family.

The Dragonettes begrudgingly agreed not to eat their favorite food. They too understood the importance of keeping their mother's word to the insects that flew around the Singular Oak.

Fortunately for the Dragonettes, there was indeed plenty of other food in the form of mushrooms, meat trees, which are a particular form of tree, only in Oz, that bears meat as its fruit like an apple tree bears apples, and the rock moss that grows on the rocks in the nearby stream which feeds the Munchkin River from Lake Nogard.

They were after all, growing Dragonettes who were now reaching their early teen years, having passed one hundred years of age and their tastes were changing.

For Drago and Dragonelli, the next few hundred years were going to be rough as the Dragonettes begin to spread out and try new things, like flying and testing their flames.

Aadon Blu enjoyed the Pinwheel Raft from one of the canvas seats as Darlene pedaled the odd contraption nearly as fast as Aadon had done the day before. He marveled at the speed as they leapt across the borders of Winkie Country and into the mostly purple landscape of Gillikin Country.

Within a couple of hours of steady pedaling, Darlene spied the Pinwheel Fields off in the far distance to the east and increased her pace… just a bit.

In the span of a few minutes, the Pinwheel Raft crossed the purple prairie grasses and was now coming to a halt beside a small house at the entranceway into the Pinwheel Fields.

A large purple spider name Boris, according to Aadon, who was both happy to be home and sad to leave new friends behind.

Heavenlee assured Aadon that they would see much more of each other as the years pass.

Hugs and kisses were in great abundance as the friends parted company, leaving Aadon Blu standing on the porch of his home, and waving farewell to the Pinwheel Raft and its occupants.

"You are never going to believe the adventure I had up in the Dark Forest of Gillikin Country while you were riding that thing with a spinning pinwheel on it, playing around and abandoning your post," Boris exclaimed as they enter the doorway into their shared home.

Aadon Blu rolled his eyes and proceeded to explain the last few days to his friend and Co-Caretaker of the Pinwheel Fields.

As the Pinwheel Raft headed in a generally southeast direction towards the soft green glow of Emerald City, Heavenlee looked down at the runners of the Pinwheel Raft, where the Snot Otters were sliming great volumes of slime and ooze.

"What about the Snot Otters? Don't they get to go home?" she asked her mother.

Darlene thought for a moment. In all the commotion, they had forgotten about the Snot Otters. An idea slowly came to her as she pondered the dilemma of the Snot Otters.

"We shall ask Princess Ozma to send them home. Being so kind as She is, I'm certain they will find their way home through Her.

Heavenlee scurried about the Pinwheel Raft, speaking to each Snot Otter; asking them if they wanted to go home now or later, when they arrived in Emerald City.

Since no Snot Otter had ever visited Emerald City before, each of them jumped at the chance without hesitation. They would return with wondrous stories that captivated the Snot Otters for years to come.

In no time, the Pinwheel Raft had passed the western edge of the Great Southern Gillikin Mountains and was soon in Munchkin Country, headed towards the ever-growing green glow of Emerald City.

The countryside had taken on a decidedly blue hue, or so Mr. Tinker noticed from his perch atop the odd looking pedaling contraption. He recalled that blue was the color of Munchkin Country and most everything in it, just as Quadling Country, where Glinda; Good Witch of the South was Ruler, was mostly red, including Glinda's Red Brick Palace.

By mid-afternoon, the Pinwheel Raft had crossed into Emerald Country and soon was slowly entering the Eastern Gate of Emerald City, surrounded by throngs of citizens, all eager to see the new contraption that had arrived.

Princess Ozma greeted the Pinwheel Raft as it came to a stop at the Gates of the Palace of Princess Ozma.

Mr. Tinker had ceased his pedaling and was suddenly awestruck by the radiance of the Royal Monarch. He could recall, with great effort, the small infant that had been Princess Ozma when She was born of King Pastoria and Queen Lurline, who was an immortal fairy creature.

He remembered how She cooed and cried when She was but a baby and he had not seen Her mature into a Ruler of Oz.

Now, this fairy creature of pure Love and radiance was standing before the Pinwheel Raft, bearing greetings and well wishes.

Princess Ozma rejoiced as Heavenlee and her mother, Darlene disembarked from the Pinwheel Raft and embraced the Royal Ruler of Oz.

They introduced Mr. Tinker, whom Princess Ozma remembered faintly from her earliest childhood.

"Your Majesty," Mr. Tinker declared as he bowed low before the Princess.

The Princess smiled, Her face beaming with confidence and an almost child-like quality. She may have looked to be about sixteen years of age, but Princess Ozma had been around as long as the Land of Oz. Her wisdom was naturally won and well-used. For more than a hundred years, the Land of Oz lived an idyllic Life; and as long as the Princess ruled over the fairy lands of Oz, it would continue to do so.

The rest of the day was spent in festive gatherings and with an abundance of food and refreshments about.

The Snot Otters asked to stay around a while when Princess Ozma offered to send them home.

Being a benevolent Ruler, She provided a fine bed of long, smooth rocks in a fast-flowing small stream that Princess Ozma created, which spanned the length of the Palace Gardens, to the rear of the Palace... and the four Snot Otters were quite content to stay around for a while.

Darlene and Heavenlee returned to their home in Emerald City, where Darlene's mate, Hank, and his son Buddy were working hard on the day's business at their shop, called Hank & Buddy's Joke and Gag Gift Shop.

It took Darlene and Heavenlee several days to get over the excitement of the adventure they had set out upon almost a month ago.

Fortunately, Hank and Buddy were very patient in listening to their stories of Dragons and Dragonflies, Nomes and gnome, as well as Snot Otters and a Pinwheel Raft.

For several weeks, Emerald City was abuzz about the return of the Nomes. Many knew how calamitous it could have been had the last Nome in Oz escaped and nearly all were glad they had returned.

Mr. Tinker had joined forces with several of Princess Ozma's jewelers and gem smiths in order to produce a setting worthy of the Lunar Gems. As they labored on his design, he enlisted the aid of the Sawhorse and Princess Ozma' Big Red Wagon for an overnight journey back to Roy G Bivopolis. It was an uneventful journey, which Mr. Tinker was most grateful for. He had had enough of adventure... at least for a while.

When he returned, the Big Red Wagon was loaded down with Enarc Brenkert, the block of Fluviam, and all seven Roy G Biv's.

Chapter 59
A Gift of Lunar Gems

Jamie Diggs read the invitation that had been brought by Messenger Crow, all the way from Emerald City.

It came in an envelope, being wrapped with a gold ribbon and was clearly a Royal Invitation, especially when he saw the wax seal of Oz on the back.

The Royal Magician of Oz read the words carefully and with great interest.

Come witness Enarc Brenkert
The Wonder of Oogaboo
Summer Solstice
Sundown
The Palace of Princess Ozma

"Will you be attending?" the Messenger Crow asked. "Her Majesty requests a response."

"Of course, you silly bird!" Jamie replied.

It had been several weeks since his adventure with Heavenlee and Aadon. Rumor had reached his home that something special was in the planning at Princess Ozma's Royal Palace and Mr. Tinker had something to do with it.

James, Amanda and Oscar Diggs were delighted to attend a Royal Function and the days passed slowly until the Summer Solstice, still a month away.

As Time always does, it passed one moment at a time until it was the afternoon of the Summer Solstice.

By now, the anticipation across Oz was at a fever pitch. It seems everyone knew about the Royal Performance, or was it a Royal Ball?

Only Mr. Tinker and Her Majesty knew all the details, and they weren't "spilling the beans," as Mr. Tinker liked to say.

The Handmaidens and other staff at the Royal Palace were flawless in their preparations for the event, which was a marvel since they had no idea what was going to happen either.

Soon, friends and invited guests were gathering in the Great Hall, where a large number of seats had been assembled, all facing towards a silver screen.

Behind the seats was the strangest contraption anyone outside of a select few had any idea what it was.

Everyone walked by it and stared at the words

that were clearly visible on the back of it. No one had a clue what, or who Enarc Brenkert was, and the mystery of it made the evening's anticipation that much more enjoyable.

Jamie Diggs and his family arrived, just before sundown, by means of the Magic Door, which Princess Ozma was more than happy to open for him.

"So wonderful of you to attend Mr. Tinker's Grand Event," Princess Ozma declared. She embraced everyone warmly and led them towards the strange contraption.

They looked over the strange contraption with some familiarity. James looked at Amanda, then at Jamie, who was looking back at them. Oscar also seemed strangely familiar with the strange contraption.

It was Jamie who broke the silence of the moment.

"We're gonna watch a movie?" he asked.

Princess Ozma smiled warmly, but had no idea what a 'movie' was.

"What did you say?" Mr. Tinker chimed in, having overheard them from his seat next to Enarc Brenkert.

"That's a movie projector, so it makes sense that we're..." Jamie started to explain.

"It says inside that it's a motion picture projector," Mr. Tinker interrupted. "Have you seen one of these before?"

Jamie rolled his eyes.

"Of course we have! We've been to lots of movies," he replied.

Mr. Tinker looked at James and Amanda, who both nodded in agreement.

James explained about how people in the Great Outside sat in darkened theaters, watching movies about things no one in Oz had any knowledge of.

"I just love movie popcorn!" Amanda exclaimed.

Princess Ozma chuckled softly, amused by Mr. Tinker's reactions to James and Amanda stories. Hearing Amanda's declaration gave Her an idea and She called for a Handmaiden and whispered in her ear.

The Handmaiden was off to the kitchen on her Royal Errand when the clarion calls of trumpets sounded, heralding the setting sun of the Summer Solstice.

Anyone who was anyone in the Land of Oz was present for the Wonder of Oogaboo and what it would do.

Seated together in the front row were the Scarecrow, Tin Woodman, Cowardly Lion and Jack Pumpkinhead.

Scattered about were Aunt Em and Uncle Henry, with Dorothy and Toto nearby.

Glinda: Good Witch of the South had chosen a seat next to Princess Ozma, as was her custom.

Heavenlee and Darlene, who were joined by Hank and Buddy, found a nice set of seats next to Aadon Blu and a group of four Snot Otters.

Jamie and his family sat next to them, near the movie projector and wondered how the thing worked; especially since the Land of Oz had no electricity to speak of, other than the occasional lightning bolt.

It was Oscar Diggs who pointed out the large block of copper and zinc that was positioned behind the strange contraption and seemed to be connected in some way to Enarc Brenkert.

"I do believe that is called Fluviam, if I am not mistaken?" the former Wizard of Oz suggested.

"Fluviam? Amanda inquired.

When O.Z. Diggs had been carried away by the balloon, leaving Dorothy and Toto behind in Emerald City, he had eventually returned to the Great Outside and spent some time there before returning to Oz to live out his days.

As such, he had seen the rise of Thomas Edison and Nicholas Tesla, so he understood what Fluviam actually was.

"It produces electricity, just like a battery," he explained to everyone within earshot.

No one there had a clue what electricity, or even a battery was, except for the Diggs family, who all nodded their heads and smiled.

Once more, the trumpets sounded and everyone took their seats, including Princess Ozma.

Mr. Tinker stood up and thanked everyone for attending. He came forward and retrieved a necklace from a small white pouch that he had been carrying with him all day.

"When I made my journey to the Moon, it was to gather stars for King Pastoria's crown, but the beauty of the place compelled me to abandon Oz and make my home there, among the craters and plains of grey rock and gray dirt. For more than a hundred years, I was content, until I learned that Life was more than the stark beauty of grey on gray. The lessons of the rainbow on the dark side of the Moon taught me well and I longed for the color, and the joy, and the mystery that is the Land of Oz. I also wanted to visit my old home in Evna, across the Impassable Desert in the Land of Ev and find my old partner, Mr. Smith," the little tinker from Ev said longingly. "I came to the Moon for the stars, but instead, found these Lunar Gems, which I would have presented to your father, King Pastoria, were he still among us today."

Princess Ozma applauded softly, joined by virtually everyone in the Great Hall, many of whom remembered well the benevolent King Pastoria and his daughter, Princess Ozma.

"And now, I present them to you, Your Majesty, as the rightful heir to the Lunar Gems" he announced as he bowed low and slow.

The Princess approached Mr. Tinker, who placed the Lunar Gems, now encased in a stunning silver necklace, around her graceful neck.

The effect was amazing as the Lunar Gems glowed bright orange, with brilliant rays of orange light extending outwards towards the gathering of people and creatures and such.

Jack Pumpkinhead seemed particularly pleased since his favorite color was orange.

Aunt Em, Amanda and Darlene fawned over the necklace, stunned by its raw beauty and exotic glow.

"And now, let the story of Dorothy and her arrival in Oz begin!" Mr. Tinker announced as he flipped the switch on Enarc Brenkert.

Chapter 60
More Popcorn Please

The Handmaidens passed out bowls of popcorn to everyone who wanted some. Princess Ozma was very pleased that Her own surprise was being received so well. There was great excitement as Enarc Brenkert lit up and began whirring and clicking while the two reels spun slowly.

"Turn it up!" Jamie shouted. "We can't hear a thing!"

James agreed, as did Amanda.

"Yea, we can't hear the sound," they both said together.

Mr. Tinker flipped the switch and Enarc Brenkert went dark and silent, causing an audible groan throughout the audience.

"What do you mean, 'turn it up'?" he asked. "What sound?"

James tried to explain to Mr. Tinker about how there should be sound, but to no avail. The little tinker from Ev didn't understand.

"Are you telling me that Enarc Brenkert speaks?" he asked the Diggs family.

Jamie rolled his eyes, as did James and Amanda.

"Sort of. It's just that there should be talking... and sometimes music," Jamie explained.

James could tell that Mr. Tinker was not quite understanding the concept of a talking motion picture.

"There should be speakers that hook up to this thing and sound comes out of them," he explained.

All the while, the crowd was getting restless and was ready for Enarc Brenkert to resume its story of Dorothy and the Wizard of Oz.

"Can you show me how to make these things you call speakers?" Mr. Tinkers asked James and his son.

Princess Ozma, who had been watching and listening, called for the Royal Orchestra to play some music while Mr. Tinker and James made for the workshop that was once Oscar's and was now Jamie's.

Within an hour, they returned with two wooden boxes, each equipped with a paper cone on one side and a tail of copper wire coming out of the back of the other side.

"This is kinda crude, but is should work," James assured the audience, who were thoroughly enjoying the musical performance.

Mr. Tinker attached the copper wires from the two boxes into several spots on the black box of Enarc Brenkert and stepped back to admire their work.

He rewound the film and flipped the switch once more.

Enarc Brenkert roared to Life as a lion appeared on the silver screen in front of them all.

Everyone in attendance, including the Diggs family, were captivated by the 'movie', as the Royal Magician of Oz had called it.

When Dorothy sang her song, there were tears among many in the audience.

They hissed and booed when the old woman took away Toto and cheered when he escaped from the basket.

They laughed at Professor Marvel and were genuinely frightened when the tornado struck and carried Dorothy's house away.

Glinda was very amused when She appeared and the Munchkins sang their song about the Yellow Brick Road.

"I'm not the Good Witch of the North," Glinda observed. She leaned over towards the Princess, who was enjoying Her bowl of popcorn.

"My dress isn't that big, is it?" She asked the Princess, who nodded politely.

As each of the three companions of Dorothy appeared, there was a general cheer of approval and a wave of hisses whenever the Wicked Witch of the West appeared.

There was a huge gasp of amazement when the Wizard of Oz's flaming head appeared and commanded the four friends, and Toto too, to retrieve the broomstick of the Wicked Witch of the West.

Oscar Diggs excused himself during that part as he was too embarrassed by the whole thing. He returned in time to watch the Flying Monkeys capture of Dorothy and Toto.

By the time Enarc Brenkert had reached the part where Dorothy had returned to her home in Kansas, a murmur ran through the audience.

There was much debate about Kalidahs, Field Mice and Witches as everyone chimed in with their opinions regarding the Wonder of Oogaboo.

Soon, all eyes were on Dorothy, who had remained silent throughout the performance.

"That was wonderful!" she exclaimed. "Can we see it again?"

Everyone in the audience was in complete agreement and Princess Ozma called for an encore.

It took Mr. Tinker no more than a few minutes rewind the film for a repeat performance.

As they waited, Jamie Diggs visited with his dear friend, Princess Dorothy, who he had met and became friends with during his first journey to Oz.

They were joined by the Scarecrow, Tin Woodman and the Cowardly Lion.

Each of them were amazed by Enarc Brenkert and his telling of the tale of Dorothy's arrival in Oz.

"Exactly so! I am a humbug."

"It's not quite the way I remember it happening," the Scarecrow observed.

"But it's close enough and it's a wonderful way to tell the story," Dorothy replied. "Besides, I love the music!"

"Ladies and gentlemen! Intermission is concluded! Please take your seats for the encore performance of Enarc Brenkert!" Mr. Tinker announced.

In a matter of moments, the Great Hall went silent as everyone took their seats and awaited the encore.

Once again, Mr. Tinker flipped the switch to bring Enarc Brenkert to Life, so to speak.

"More popcorn please," Princess Ozma asked a nearby Handmaiden, who rushed off and was back moments later with a heaping bowl of freshly popped popcorn, sprinkled with melted butter and black pepper, Her Majesty's favorite.

The End